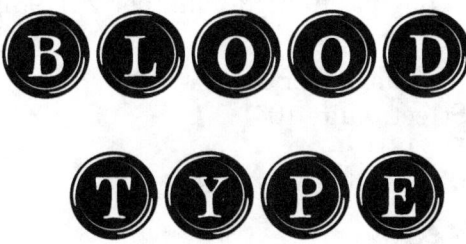

BLOOD TYPE

JULIE KENT

ISBN 978-1-62806-142-0   (print | paperback)
ISBN 978-1-62806-143-7   (print | hardback)

Library of Congress Control Number 2017961210

Published by Salt Water Media
29 Broad Street, Suite 104
Berlin, MD 21811
www.saltwatermedia.com

Cover design by Anita Dawn Blevins

To my husband, Larry:

You have been with
me through everything.

Thank you, my love.

In the quiet night,
in the dark silence of the bedroom
my anger became fear...

— *Edgar Allan Poe*

CARISSA

...was all that was displayed on the page when Old Lady Parrish returned to her desk from her shower. She could only stare at the single sheet of white paper protruding from the top of her typewriter as her eyes burned and filled with tears. Her hands quickly moved to cover her mouth as she gasped and shook as her body was completely stricken with terror.

"NOOO!" She screamed at the machine. "That's not right! What did you do?" She sobbed and pleaded as if she was going to get an answer. Her entire face fell into her hands as she dropped to her knees. "Please take it back! Oh my God! PLEASE TAKE IT BACK!" She screamed, but she knew her pleas were not going to change anything. There was nothing she could do. Nothing...

After crying hysterically on the floor for a few minutes, she stood up and began to frantically pace back and forth across her bedroom. Things did *not* go the way she planned. She continued to cry as she searched for answers as to what she could do. *How could she fix this? Was it too late?* She kept asking herself these questions over and over again, but she already knew the answers. The problem could *not* be fixed because it *was* too late.

Mrs. Parrish became enraged and knew she had

to do something. She went into her closet to look for something that would help her release her anger, and in her fit of rage, she started pulling her clothes off the hangers and throwing them all over the floor. She picked up several pairs of shoes as well as the clothes that were strewn all over the closet floor and threw them outside the closet door until her bedroom was so covered she could barely see the mahogany hardwood floor anymore. A bead of sweat dripped into her eye as she turned to pick up the last thing she could possibly throw, a pair of snow boots. She reached for them and that's when she saw it, the answer to her problem, or at least she thought.

She had forgotten about the crowbar. She left it in the closet the day she pried the Royal typewriter out of its crate. Her eyes widened as she slowly reached into the corner and picked up the curved piece of steel with both hands. It was cold to the touch, but she barely noticed the way it felt in her grasp as she turned to face the opening that lead out of the closet and into her bedroom. She did not take her eyes off her shaking hands as she inched closer and closer to the doorway. The room was so cold that her hands began to shiver uncontrollably and for just one second, she almost lost her grip on what was soon to be her salvation, but she refused to let it drop. She quickly regained her composure and proceeded toward the closet doorway.

The typewriter was right where she left it, on the desk with that same single sheet of paper sticking out of it, the one that spelled out her friend's demise. As she stepped over the heap of clothing, she immediately felt a cold breeze pass by her. It was so cold in her bedroom she could see her breath with each exhale as she made her way over the piles of dresses and shoes to the middle of the floor where her solid oak desk held the Royal that, at this moment, she despised and wished she had never found.

As she glared at the piece of machinery that had made her life a living hell over the last few months, she knew she had the only solution in her hand. She reached back over her head with her right arm while holding the crowbar so tight that even though she was so cold, perspiration had formed in her hand making it difficult to maintain her grip on the bar. She grabbed the end of it with her other hand to get a better hold on it before pulling it down with everything she had inside of her and smashing it straight into the center of the keyboard of the demon before her. Realizing the impact barely made a dent in the typewriter with only the "H" and "J" keys falling through the center making a small hole in the keyboard, she swung her arms back to land a second blow, which came down right next to the hole she had already created. This time, the crowbar went right through the keys and hit the desk below. She continued to smash the crowbar into the machine over and over again as keys, pieces of the roller, and debris from the base of it flew everywhere. Mrs. Parrish did not seem to be in control of her own body anymore as she continued to destroy every mechanism within the Royal and her desk until, suddenly, her arm stopped in midair.

She stood frozen for a moment until, with one sudden blow, her bedroom window smashed and hundreds of tiny pieces of glass flew into her room and fell onto the floor around her.

She looked at the window and then back at the broken typewriter and she noticed there was still one thing intact on that desk, the paper with the letters on it. She tried to reach for it but could not move. Something held her back as she attempted to collect that fateful piece of paper so she could rip it to shreds.

She was still trying to move when the cold wind funneled in through the window and the bits of typewriter started to move. Mrs. Parrish thought the wind was causing them to flutter a little on the desktop, but she became terrified as she watched the Royal's broken pieces start to elevate themselves above the desk. Before she had time to react, the cool breeze picked up the fragments of the typewriter, along with the glass from the floor and before she knew it, she was in a tornado of debris that lifted her off the floor and moved her slowly toward her window. She tried to scream but nothing came out. She could not move. She could not speak. It moved her closer and closer to the window before a sudden burst of air and glass picked her up and threw her out of the third-floor window, dropping her to her death.

An immediate stillness took over the air and the bedroom as the Royal typewriter sat assembled on a beautiful desk of solid oak in the third-floor bedroom of Isobel Parrish's home.

As the flashes between dark and light were visible behind her closed eyelids, Chloe's eyes developed a flickering sensation which slowly brought her back to reality. She had fallen asleep to avoid the grueling hour car ride to nowhere. She was leaving one dark life filled with loneliness and bullying just to enter a new life filled with what was sure to be the same. As her eyes slowly opened, she watched the trees pass by her window as the family Ford Explorer entered a new town in a new county with new but the same sort of judgmental people she had grown accustomed to back in Clairemont. The move to Hollow Creek was a choice that was made for her, and one she could not do anything about - like every other decision made by her parents. The idea of moving into a new house in a different neighborhood was bad enough, but the thought of meeting and dealing with new people was torturous. She was quite content with the neighbors she did not like at the last place as well as her non-existent friends at crappy Clairemont High where she was forced to interact with teachers and students she despised; all of these factors aided in her achievement of a lonely, nonsocial life.

She worked hard to accomplish her lifestyle and she was happy, although she didn't look it with her dark, gloomy appearance all the time. Chloe Mattson was a seventeen-year-old introverted "Goth girl" as they called her back in Clairemont, and she was not keen on having to start all over to obtain her reputation. Chloe dressed in dark clothing (mostly black) and listened to heavy metal music. Her favorite band was The Pretty Reckless, whose lead singer, Taylor Momsen, represented everything Chloe wanted to be. She dressed like her, wore heavy dark make-up like her, and listened to her music all the time. Chloe tried to only maintain one friend at a time because she thought having friends was too much work. This move was happening in the summer of 2016, just before her senior year of high school, which only added to her animosity toward her father and step-mother and resulted in the loss of the one friend she had back home, Zach. There was no way she would be able to see him now because neither of them had cars. Another thing Chloe avoided was having girls as friends because she didn't want that drama in her life. Her one friend was usually one of the opposite sex.

William Mattson, Chloe's father, who she called Bill instead of Dad ever since her mom died three years ago, was driving at a pace which made it feel like they would never get there. His wife, Sarah, was talking his ear off (slowing them down, as usual) as he just kept nodding as if he was interested in anything she was saying, but he probably didn't hear a word of it. Chloe, of course, could not hear anything they were saying to each other due to the blaring heavy metal music penetrating her brain through earbuds which ran from her iPhone straight into her eardrums. She listened to her music whenever she wanted to block the rest of the world out, which was pretty much all the time. However, on this occasion, she only needed to block out the annoying voices of Bill and Sarah, her step-mom whom she could not stand. To Chloe, listening to her was like hearing fingernails running along a chalk board, so she really hoped Sarah would not be one of her teachers at the new school. The reason for uprooting the family and moving them to a new town was Sarah's fault; as a high school English teacher, she was offered a job at Hollow Creek High in the great new town of Hollow Creek. Chloe had been able to dodge this bullet so far, but this year, Sarah was going to be teaching at the senior level.

Chloe continued to stare out the window, expressionless until her gaze into the air was interrupted by something cool and wet nudging her arm. It was her dog, Raven, trying to get her attention as she pushed her face onto Chloe's lap. Raven was her true best friend, always there for Chloe no matter what. She was a beautiful German Sheppard who loved Chloe just as much as Chloe loved her. Raven rode in the back seat with her and, like Chloe, she slept the entire ride until now. Raven looked up into the sunlight that was coming in through the car window. She displayed the most beautiful shade of red mixed with black that was on her back, down her nose, and on the tips of her ears. Her fur was so soft and Chloe could just sit and pet her for hours, which seemed to be therapeutic for both of them. Raven was the only constant in Chloe's life. Sarah didn't care about anyone but herself, Bill was always working, and Chloe's real mom, Carissa was dead. Raven was all she had, which was fine with her. It was going to be interesting to see how things with Bill were going to work out with this move. He was an auto mechanic and had his own shop back in Clairemont, which took many years of his hard work to acquire. The plan was to move the Hollow Creek and he would commute two hours for work. Chloe dreaded this: his long drive home would keep him from getting home at a decent hour which meant she would be spending a lot of time alone with her stepmother.

The Explorer stopped at a traffic light and Bill looked back at Chloe, saying something to her but all she could see was the awkward movement of his lips and bobbing of his head. She could not hear and did not care what he was saying. He reached back and tapped her on the knee, which signaled her to remove the earbuds for a moment because he obviously felt like he had something important to say. She removed the right earbud, allowing her music to continue to blare into her left ear while her father pointed out the passenger side window. Raven lifted her head from Chloe's lap and the two of them looked in the direction Bill pointed.

"Look Chloe. That is where you will be going to school," Bill said with a slight smile even though he knew she didn't care. "It doesn't look so bad," he said as he watched her replace her earbud.

Chloe continued to listen to the singing of the only person she felt really understood her at this point in her life. Momsen sang her big hit "My Medicine" into Chloe's ears as she gave her father an annoyed look.

Bill just nodded his head and started to drive again as the light turned green.

Chloe didn't care about the school, the town, the people, or the new house they were moving into which was really not new at all. It was built back in the 50s and was probably falling apart. She didn't know because she hadn't seen it yet. That was actually her fault because she refused to go with Bill and Sarah whenever they went to look at it. The only thing of interest for Chloe about this whole move was the fact that she heard someone may have died in their new house. The idea of a possible ghost fascinated her as she tried to maintain the appearance of one herself. Apparently, the house had been on the market for a while and her father worked out a pretty good deal for it because of this minor "death" detail.

Apparently, it's not easy to sell a house someone may have died in.

It was December 21, 2013 and Carissa Mattson was getting ready for her annual company Christmas party. The real estate company she worked for usually went all out for the event with a catered, four-course meal with an open bar. She and Bill had been arguing that entire day. Their disagreement turned into a screaming match just before it was time to leave for the party so Carissa told Bill she did not want him to go. She said he would ruin her evening. To avoid any further display of altercation in front of Chloe, Bill agreed to drive her there, drop her off, and pick her up when the party was over. Carissa agreed as she went into her daughter Chloe's room and kissed her goodbye. That would be the last time Chloe saw her mother.

Carissa was killed in a car accident that cold, snowy December night on her way home. Bill had gone back to pick her up later that evening. Carissa didn't do any of the driving because she was planning on doing a lot of drinking, which she had successfully done. She was the passenger in the car and they were t-boned in the middle of an intersection due to Bill running a red light. A pickup truck slammed into the passenger side of their Jeep Wrangler which caused it to roll onto its side, throwing Carissa out of the windshield. She was not wearing her seatbelt. Chloe has blamed all of the wrongs in her life, especially her mom's death, on her father since that day. After all, he was the one driving the car. He wasn't even at the Christmas party with her because she was mad at him and told him not to come. She got completely intoxicated because of him so he had to pick her up because she couldn't drive.

It was about 1:00 a.m. when the police officer rang the doorbell of the Mattson home. Chloe was home alone and hesitantly opened the door to an officer taking off his hat. He asked her to get dressed (she was in her pajamas) and he would take her to the hospital to see her father, who had just been in an accident. He did not mention Carissa at all and Chloe was too afraid to ask. She quickly put on some boots and a coat and the officer drove her to Clairemont Memorial Hospital where he led her in through the emergency entrance and into Room 4 where Bill was lying with bandages on his right arm and left leg. He had scrapes and bruises on his face and he had obviously been crying.

Chloe ran over to him and wrapped her arms around him. "Dad!" She was trembling. "What happened? Where's Mom?"

Bill hugged her with his one good arm and started to sob. "I'm so sorry, Chloe," he said softly. "I love you. I'm so sorry. Your mom..." he stopped abruptly as if he was searching for the words. Just then, a nurse came in the room to take his vital signs.

"I'm so sorry about your loss," she said to him. Then she looked at Chloe. "I'm so sorry, sweetie," she said as she walked out of the room.

"Dad, what is she talking about?" Chloe began to cry because she knew she still hadn't seen her mom anywhere. "Where's Mom?"

"Chlo Bear," he started. (He called her that when she was younger.) "The road was slippery. The truck came out of nowhere." He looked down into her eyes. "She didn't make it, Bear. I'm so sorry. It was my fault!" He cried.

"NOOO!" Chloe screamed and ran out of the room. Things had not been the same between her and Bill since that day. That was when Chloe's entire world was turned upside down and she started to change.

The Mattson family turned onto Honeysuckle Drive, a road where the street was lined with old Victorian-style houses, each with its own distinct color and architectural design. Some of the homes had porches that seemed to circle the entire house; others had porch swings and plants on the steps that lead up to their front door. These beautiful homes intrigued Chloe as she sat up in the back seat of the Explorer to look out the window and get a better view. Bill drove the car slowly as the family looked around the neighborhood that was to be their new home.

Chloe could not believe how enchanting the street looked. The houses were so perfectly designed they looked like gingerbread houses. One of the homes was blue with white trim around its large rounded bay windows while the pillars that seemed to be holding it up were red. One was brick red with green trim that surrounded the windows, but its pillars were beige, while the house next to it was yellow with blue trim. That home had the most amazing roof that had a round octagonal tower-looking thing that came to a steep point. All of the houses had two, three, or four stories and had several rounded, bay windows.

One thing Chloe started to notice was the lack of people. She didn't see any kids playing outside or dogs being walked. There were cars in some of the driveways so she knew people were there. It was during the day so she just figured everyone was at work until she did see a young man retrieving his mail out of his mailbox before he quickly turned to walk back up to what she assumed was his home. Bill slowed the car down to a crawl right in front of the man's house and Chloe's heart skipped a beat. "What are you doing?" she asked, almost in a shout.

"This is us," he said as he pulled in the next driveway which wrapped all the way around a three-story Victorian house that was red with black outlines that surrounded the large bay windows and a black, wooden railing on the steps that lead to the front door. From a distance, it appeared to be made of brick due to its color, but as they pulled closer to the front door, one could see it was constructed of shingles.

"What do you think?" Bill asked as he turned to look at his daughter who was still listening to her music while straining her neck to get a better view of the house. He tapped her leg and she turned to him and took one of her earbuds out. "Well? What do you think?"

Chloe opened her car door and looked up at one of the windows on the third floor and nonchalantly said, "Whatever," as she stepped out onto the driveway trying not to show any enthusiasm at all, even though she was in awe of the sheer size and beauty of their new home. Raven jumped out and stayed right by her side. Chloe gave her a treat that she had in her pocket for being such a good girl during the car ride, which Raven devoured before running onto the front lawn to relieve herself.

"The movers should be here soon so why don't we go in and look around?" Bill glanced at Chloe, "You can have your room picked out before they get here."

Chloe opened her car door again to get out a suitcase she had packed for herself, just in case the movers did not get there in a timely fashion. She set the suitcase down on the ground and made sure she had her iPhone safely in her pocket with her earbuds. She reached down to pick it up and turned to go to the front door of the house where Bill and Sarah were waiting for her. She didn't know why, but they insisted on going into their new home all together, which Chloe thought was so corny and stupid. She proceeded slowly to the front stairway and along the way she glanced back up at that same window that caught her attention upon their arrival. There was a glare from the sun shining on the glass that made her squint. She was just about to turn her attention to the front door when something caught her eye. She strained to see beyond the glare and could swear there was someone standing in that window. She quickly shut her eyes and reopened them thinking that would help her get a better look. The image was gone. She was sure she saw someone, but then she had just had a long car ride and was tired. She convinced herself that had to be it, but then she remembered the reason they got this amazing house for such a great price and the thought of someone or something being in that window was not that farfetched, was it?

Bill fumbled for the key on his key ring and proceeded to open the front door when Chloe finally walked up the front steps. He slowly opened the door as if it were the grand opening to a new business or something. When the door opened enough and they could see inside, the idea of this being the grand opening of something felt a little more real.

The foyer gave entryway into the house which was wall to wall hardwood flooring that lead to a stairway just on the right and a living and dining area straight ahead. The wooden stairs where railed with a white banister which had a pedestal at the bottom. The inside of the house was just as beautiful as the outside. Even the walls were a deep maroon color and there was a small black chandelier with glass votive candle-like lights in the entryway, which gave the home an instant Gothic look. The house had been closed up for a while so it did have a sort-of musty smell, but that seemed to only go along with its motif.

Their footsteps and voices echoed throughout the house and Chloe immediately made her way to the staircase. She and Raven climbed the stairs together slowly. Chloe was looking up the entire time as she could see straight up onto the other floors through the open floor plan. There were three floors and she intended to go all the way up in order to locate the bedroom which would keep her the furthest away from the Bill and Sarah.

When she got to the third floor there was a loft or something at the top of the stairs with a bathroom right next to it. There was a long dark hallway with a closed door at the end. Chloe and Raven made their way to that door and opened it. On the other side of it was a large room with a single rounded bay window. There was hardwood floor with a walk-in closet to her right and she knew she found her room. She looked around and walked over to the window to look out. She knew this room would give her the seclusion she so craved. She also knew whatever she saw was in that window. "What do you think Raven?" The dog's ears perked up as soon as Chloe spoke as if she understood and was giving approval.

Downstairs, she could hear her father and Sarah rooting around and making plans for what piece of furniture would go where. In the end, it would all depend on what Sarah wanted because she always got her way with Bill. Chloe didn't even know why they were having a conversation about such things as Sarah had already made up her mind and that was all that mattered.

The loud rumble of the moving truck was finally heard outside as it backed into the driveway. Chloe saw Bill and Sarah go outside to meet the movers and start pointing and talking. Chloe could not hear, nor did she care, what they were saying, but she knew the next couple of hours would be full of Sarah barking orders at the movers and her father as they would jump into action and place every bit of furniture exactly where she wanted it to be. Chloe couldn't for the life of her, figure out why her father put up with that. They had only been married for about a year and she demanded they move out of the house that held all of the memories of Bill and his deceased wife Carissa because she wanted to start fresh with him. That was the real reason for this move and Chloe knew it.

"Chloe, come down here!" Bill hollered up the stairway.

She didn't want to go, but she answered, "Coming!" as she hesitantly made her way down the stairs to the chaos that was happening between the movers and her step-mom while her father was going insane. He looked at her with a confused look on his face. It was no wonder with all the orders Sarah was giving everyone.

"Go outside and let them know which stuff is yours and which bedroom you would like it put into," he said.

"Alright," Chloe said. At least he was letting her pick out her own room, regardless of what Queen Sarah thought. She knew Sarah would probably have something to say about it so she knew she had to hurry up and get moved into her newly found bedroom before it could be taken away.

It was simple. Chloe had a bed, a small dresser, a night table, and a small desk, all of which were moved into her room within an hour as she quickly unpacked her two suitcases and emptied their contents into their appropriate places. She was completely moved in before her father even knew which bedroom he and the dragon lady would share.

The next four or five hours were filled with men going in and out of the house with tables, chairs, pictures, boxes, and everything else from their old house. Chloe stayed upstairs while this took place. All she could hear was the sound of the doors opening and closing, furniture sliding across the wooden floor, and Sarah's winey voice giving orders to everyone. "Watch the floor!" she said to them. "Don't scratch it before we get a chance to enjoy it."

The unmade bed in Chloe's room was good enough for her to sit on while all of this took place. She had no idea where the sheets were and did not want to go downstairs to find out. She knew if she did, she would be put to work, and she knew she did not want to get tangled in that mess. She just sat on her bed with her laptop, which she made sure to keep with her in the car. She tried to pick up someone's network so she could get online and actually entertain herself for a while, but she was unable to accomplish this. She thought either they were in a dead zone or everyone kept their networks secure.

With nothing else to do at this point, she closed her computer, lied down on the bare mattress and drifted off to sleep with Raven at her side.

5

The soft tapping on her new bedroom door was the sound that woke Chloe up from a much-needed nap. She rubbed her eyes and then tried to focus on her watch. She could barely see anything in her dusk lit room, but the light from her digital watch told her it was 7:37 in the evening. She had slept for a few hours. She heard Bill's soft voice from the other side of the door.

"Clo Bear?" he asked as if she might not be in the bedroom. She really hated it when he called her that. She wasn't four years old anymore. "Want to come down for some pizza?"

She sat up in the bed and realized she still did not have any sheets on it and she had no idea where her bedside lamp was, which was why it was so dark in there. Knowing she had to find these things and start to put her bedroom together, she decided not to drag this move out any longer. She just wanted to get things feeling like home again.

"I'm not hungry," She answered. She was still half asleep. She did, however, manage to get up and open the door and saw that he looked completely exhausted. Sarah must have worn him out downstairs making sure everything was set up to her liking. "Do you know where the rest of my things are?" She asked this before

29

she looked down at the floor and noticed that someone had put a couple of boxes marked "Chloe" outside
her bedroom door while she was sleeping. Her dad just
looked at her and smiled. "Maybe I will come down for
a piece after I set up my lamp. I can't see in here." She
had second thoughts about turning down a slice or two
of pizza. God only knew when she would have another
opportunity to eat during the turmoil over the next few
days.

"OK," he said, "so, this is it, huh? This is the
room you want? It's great, Chloe." He tried to start a
little friendly conversation between them, but she just
shrugged it off.

"Yeah. It's alright." With that, she closed the door
in his face.

After getting her lamp set up and putting her favorite black sheets on her bed, Chloe finally went into
her new closet to get a feel for how she wanted to orga-
nize it. It was very spacious with two poles for hanging
clothes on and there were a lot of hangers already in
there. She didn't know where they came from and really
didn't care because what really drew her attention into
the closet further was a large wooden chest that, upon
closer view, she realized was nailed shut. She stared at
it for a few moments and could see the hammer marks
from whoever wanted it sealed tight. She noticed that
one of the nails was sticking out just enough that she
thought for sure that she would be able to pull it out
with her father's hammer. She thought it would be cool

to open this wooden box and have her own secret storage place in her closet for things she didn't want her parents to find. Not to mention, but what could have possibly been inside the thing? She just had to open it. That chest suddenly became more important than anything else at that moment. All she needed was the right tool to open it.

She decided to go downstairs for her slice of pizza (at least that's what she told Bill), but what she really wanted was to get his hammer, so she nonchalantly asked if she could borrow it.

"What for?" he asked her. Bill thought this was an odd request.

She lied: "I just need to hang some things on my wall. Don't worry, it's nothing you would not approve of." She said this sarcastically and without thinking anything of it. Maybe he just didn't want her to get upset and start an argument. He told her where his toolbox was and told her to go get it, but he urged her not to take anything else. His toolbox was his livelihood.

"Be careful. We don't want to make any ER trips on our first night in a new town," he chuckled.

Chloe ignored his joke, as she usually ignored everything he said, and went back upstairs with her pizza. She found Bill's toolbox right where he said it would be, just outside the bedroom door that was to be his and Sarah's room on the second floor. Chloe was happy with the placement of their bedroom because it was far from hers and she would be able to play her music as loud as she wanted. When she got back to her bedroom, she locked the door behind her so no one would be able to come in while she investigated the chest which she was sure no one else knew about, at least no one here in her family. This was hers and hers alone.

Before she opened the chest, she wanted to have some of her things put away so she would have something to wear the next morning. Not really caring for organization, Chloe put a few things away as she saw fit, some in the closet and some in her dresser. She did not worry about neatness. It was not really Chloe's thing. Her things were put away in less than thirty minutes and she was free to check out what she found in the closet. She took the hammer into the corner of the closet where the platform box was and sat on top of it. She secured the forked end of the hammer around the protruding nail and pulled as hard as she could. It didn't budge. She stood up so she could put her weight behind it to get more leverage and she pulled again as hard as she could and the nail finally pulled through so fast that Chloe flew backwards and hit her head on the adjacent wall. The hammer with the nail in it was still in her hand.

Raven came rushing into the closet to see what was going on. The noise startled her and she was very protective of her owner. Chloe sat there for a moment quietly petting her dog on the head because she knew she had just made a loud crashing noise that would surely have Bill running up to check on her at any moment.

She waited for two, maybe three minutes and heard nothing so she continued. She was even more eager to get into the chest than before.

There were four more nails holding the thing in place. She started to tug on the second nail; it didn't budge. Again, she pulled it with everything she had inside of her, only this time she had a tighter grip on the hammer as to not be thrown into the wall again. Still nothing. She was sweating, but continued pulling until she realized it just wasn't going to come out like the first nail. She eased her grip, let go of the hammer, and sat on the floor next to the chest with a look of defeat on her face as she stared at her opponent, the crate.

Chloe's heavy breathing started to subside as she was able to regain herself and become rested. She looked around. *Great! What do I do now?* She stood up and turned to walk out of the closet when something caught her eye. She quickly looked back and saw a crowbar in the corner of the closet right behind the chest. That was it! That was what she needed to pry the thing open. With the bar in her hand, the rest of the job would be easy.

Chloe stuck the end of the crowbar under the corner of the chest where she had been able to remove that first nail and pulled up on it. It took some strength, but one by one, the nails started coming out until they were all removed and lying on the floor at Chloe's feet. She was finally able to slowly lift the lid; however, there was so much dust covering whatever was in the box she could not make out what it was right away. The lid was so heavy it took the strength of both of her arms to lift it. She leaned the lid up on the wall next to the chest.

It was so dark inside she couldn't see a thing and there was no light in her closet, just a beam of light that cut through the closet doorway from the lamp next to her bed, which displayed all of the dust floating around in the open space. She was afraid to just reach into the darkness so she left the closet to go get her lighter out of her purse. One of Chloe's many habits that pissed off her parents was that she was a smoker. With a flick of her thumb, she was able to establish a flame that lit up the entire closet. She brought it over to the corner and held the flame slightly over the top of the box she had just opened.

There was something in the chest that was covered up by a sheet. Chloe slowly removed the sheet to reveal, what looked like a keyboard. Upon further removal of the drape, she realized it was just an old typewriter. Not just an old typewriter, an *ancient* one. It had a ribbon that was all tangled up in the keys, which were each connected (literally) to their own letter. It had a platen, she knew to be a roll that you actually had to feed paper onto through the paper feeder that it also had. This thing looked like it was in bad shape and to top it off, it was so dusty it looked gray instead of the iron black color that it was supposed to be.

Chloe reached down to lift the typewriter out of the box and was surprised by how heavy it was. She had to squat down and use all of the strength in her legs, arms, and chest to hoist it up and get it out of the top where she was only able to get it as far as the floor in the back of her closet. At least it was out and she could check it out. She couldn't help but wonder what it was doing in there and it appeared as though it was hidden. She thought it was probably just left behind because whoever moved the previous owner's belongings out of the house probably did not want to deal with how heavy the damned thing was, or they just forgot about it. Who could blame them? However, that didn't explain it being locked in the box in the closet, but it didn't matter. Chloe found something that no one else knew about and that somehow made her feel special, which was something she desperately needed.

6

Bill Mattson was an auto mechanic who owned his own shop in Clairemont. He worked for fifteen years to accomplish the ownership of his own business. He had been through several bosses and years of elbow grease while working his way up the ranks and learning the tricks of the trade. His was a small shop with only two bays, each with their own car lift. This allowed the mechanics to work in their own space. The move to Hollow Creek meant that Bill would have to commute approximately 45 minutes to work every day, which would be fine with him because it would allow him to escape the daily bickering between his wife and daughter. He enjoyed his time alone in his car. He would listen to his classic rock songs and forget about all of his stresses for a while, like the fact that he barely knew his daughter anymore, and that his wife was dead. He still referred to Carissa as his wife, however; he was careful to say "first wife" in front of the new Mrs. Mattson.

Sarah Mattson was a high school English teacher. She taught mostly ninth and tenth graders, but the upcoming school year would be different. She got a job teaching twelfth grade English and that did not make Chloe happy. There were probably a few different English faculty members at Hollow Creek High due to the broad range of options for students these days. There were the literature classes, the composition classes, and the college prep courses. Chloe knew Sarah taught literature, but did not know whether or not that would be on her schedule of classes to take. She would find out Monday when she went in to the school to get her schedule. Classes were to start on Tuesday so maybe she would have time to drop the class if she, in fact, got placed into that woman's class. Chloe did not know that much else about Sarah except that she used to sell real estate before she became a teacher. That just happened to be what Chloe's mom did for a living before her untimely death. Chloe was convinced that was one of the reasons Bill married her; maybe he was trying to duplicate his wife because she also looked like her a little bit. None of that mattered now because the damage was done and they were busy moving their belongings into the new home that had absolutely no memories of Carissa Mattson within its walls.

It was nearing 11:00 p.m. and Bill and Sarah were still putting things away in the kitchen. There were lots of fancy, breakable dishes that Bill was carefully putting into the cabinets with his wife looking over his shoulder observing his every move. There were several boxes piled on the floor that were labeled as to where they were to be put away. Five boxes were to be unloaded into the pantry while several others were specifically labeled as to what they were and where they were to go. There was one that said "cooking utensils, 3rd drawer to the left of the dishwasher." Sarah was obsessively anal-retentive and had decided where everything would go before they even got there.

All Chloe could hear was Sarah telling Bill where she wanted things as he listened and obeyed her orders. They were making a lot of noise for the sounds to travel up two stories to Chloe's ears. He knew that listening to Sarah would be a lot easier than trying to have his own opinions on anything because that would just start an argument, and it was entirely too late in the evening for that. Chloe didn't know why he put up with her. She figured it was just because he would rather have that kind of relationship than be alone, which he really was after Carissa died.

After placing the last pot on the hanging pot rack in the kitchen, Bill let out a big yawn which was his way of saying he was tired and wanted to go to bed. Sarah actually took the hint and said that they would finish tomorrow. It was Thursday and they had all weekend to finish because school didn't start up until Tuesday so they both had a few days off. At least Chloe would be starting her new school on the first day back after summer break. It was going to be hard, but it would have been more difficult if she had started in the middle of the year.

Bill went all the way upstairs and slightly cracked Chloe's door open just to check on her. She was pretending to be asleep in her bed with Raven, who was snoozing on the bed beside her. He smiled slightly, closed the door, and headed to the bedroom he would share with Sarah. Chloe opened her eyes and stared at the darkness that was her new bedroom as she gently rubbed the top of Raven's head. She rolled onto her side and was facing the walk-in closet. She left the door open, but could see nothing but complete blackness in there. Not even the moonlight that was beaming in through her window would allow her to see anything beyond her bed because that's as far as the light went, her bed. She did not have to see anything to know what was waiting for her in that closet.

As the sun rose the next morning, it was overwhelmingly brilliant as it made itself known through Chloe's window and rested directly on her cheek, warming it just a little and waking her from a dreamless sleep. This made her think about the placement of her bedroom window because she would have to figure out a way to live with the sun coming in every morning. However, she was not sure if it was the light that actually woke her up or the fact that she was freezing. She just had a quick thought about getting some dark curtains for this window before looking over the remnants of her room for something to put on, but her eyes only found their way to her watch, which was on her nightstand next to her bed. It was 6:57 am and she did not want to be awake yet, but between her shivering and Raven's nose nudging her face, she had no choice.

Chloe got out of bed, put on some slippers and a sweatshirt to cover the tank she was wearing, and patted her thigh, cueing Raven she was about to get her way and go outside. She wondered why her room was so cold. It was the beginning of September, and it was going to be another 90-degree day. This had been one of the hottest summers Chloe could remember. They went downstairs and made their way quietly to the backdoor as everyone else still slept. Chloe just looked out the back window for a moment to take in the view of their new backyard. It was enormous with plenty of space for Raven to run around. They had about a half-acre of nicely mowed grass with a treeline further back that bordered their property. She made plans in her head to go check out the wooded area later that day, but right now she opened the back door so Raven could go out and do what she needed to do. Afterwards, with a look of satisfaction on her face, Raven quickly went back into the house, and she and Chloe made their way back up to their bedroom.

Chloe decided to stay up now that she was awake so she got dressed and the first thing she wanted to do was try to get that typewriter out of her closet and onto her desk where she could get a better look at it; however, when she went over to where she left it and bent down to pick it up, she was surprised because, although it was just as heavy as she remembered, it was easier to lift than it was the previous night. She was able to slowly and carefully make it to her desk holding the solid piece of metal tightly with both hands underneath it and placed it on the top of her desk. Out of breath from the task, she plopped down in her desk chair and looked at the antique writing tool for a few moments, dreading the task of looking for some cleaning supplies in order to clean it up. She had no idea where anything was in this new house. She could clearly see how dirty and dusty it was now that it was out in the open. She had the strong urge to clean it and fix it up to get it working. It would be perfect for her Gothic theme she was planning to incorporate into her bedroom.

Before she could clean the typewriter, Chloe had to know what she was dealing with and what to use so she would not hurt it in any way. She got her laptop out, opened it, and did a search for old typewriters (apparently, someone close by left their network open). It only took a second to find out what she actually had in front of her was a Royal Typewriter which was made in the 1940s. Chloe loved the internet. She was able to find pictures and lots of information regarding the typewriter and she became more and more intrigued. Knowing she had a real antique she did not want to ruin it so she went downstairs and hunted through the medicine cabinet and linen closet hoping Bill and Sarah had put everything away in there. She was in luck because she found some dust cloths, Q-tips (which she thought would be good for cleaning between the keys), and some rubbing alcohol and Windex which she might not use because she was afraid to get the machine wet. At this point, she did not know what her fascination was with this machine; all she knew was that she *had* to get it cleaned up and fixed up to see if it worked. She brought the cleaning supplies back up to her room and immediately got to work on her newfound friend.

With supplies in hand, she quickly went to work. It was hard to clean parts of the typewriter, especially the keys, because Chloe had trouble getting the Q-tips into some of the smaller parts and crevices. The further she got into her cleaning the more she noticed about the apparatus. It was so damaged. There were scrapes all over it and the ribbon was barely recognizable. She couldn't believe people used to actually rely on these things to do any kind of writing; she lived in the computer age where everything was as easy as the click of a button.

Before she knew it, two hours had passed and she was brought back to reality by a rumbling in the pit of her stomach. She thought this would be a good time to take a break to get something to eat. She put down her dusting cloth and covered the typewriter up with the original sheet it was wrapped up in when she found it. She did not want anyone to see it if they happened to walk into her room, which she knew would never happen because she has made it clear on more than one occasion that she did not want anyone in her bedroom uninvited at any time. Well, it was clear at the old place so she figured it would be understood in the new house in Hollow Creek, or at least she hoped.

8

Downstairs, Bill and Sarah were making a late morning breakfast together. The aroma of pancakes and sausage, drifted up the steps as Chloe made her way downstairs. This was her favorite breakfast so when she reached the kitchen she asked if there was enough for her.

Sarah replied, "Of course there is, sweetie."

Chloe hated when she called her that. She made such a great effort to not be anyone's *sweetie,* especially Sarah's. "Thanks," Chloe said as she grabbed a plate out of the cupboard and sat at the table.

"How did you sleep, Chlo?" Bill asked in an attempt to start up a nice morning conversation. He knew Chloe was not a morning person or a talker for that matter, but he could not help but try. "I thought we might check out the local shopping mall and get a closer look at your school before you start on Tuesday. What do you think?"

Chloe grabbed a piece of sausage from a plate that Sarah had just put on the table, took a bite of it, looked at him and said, "Busy." With that, she grabbed another piece of sausage and gave it to Raven. Then she got up from the table and walked out of the kitchen, never even getting any pancakes. He didn't need to know what she was doing. It was not his business. Chloe and Raven went back upstairs.

"Don't worry about it, Bill." Sarah tried to comfort him. She knew he did not like the fact that Chloe never talked to him anymore. "She'll come around. Maybe this change will be good for her."

He glanced toward the direction in which Chloe walked out of the kitchen. "I hope so. I don't know, hun, she's just so angry all the time anymore."

Raven started to run up the stairs before they reached the second floor. She ran all the way up to the room she shared with Chloe. She was already familiar with the house and knew exactly where to go. Of course, she considered it to be her room also. She beat Chloe into the bedroom, sat right next to the desk, and started to growl. Chloe moved faster in order to catch up to her because she heard the noise coming from her room and knew it was out of character for Raven to growl like that. She was such a friendly dog.

When Chloe reached her room, she noticed something was not right. She could not put her finger on it right away, but she felt something was wrong. It was also very cold up there so she opened her window hoping the warm air would raise the temperature in there somewhat. She went over to Raven and started to pet her on the head. "It's okay, girl. What is it?" She knelt down beside her dog to comfort her. That was when she saw it; the typewriter was exposed. The sheet she put on it to cover it up was no longer on top of it. Instead, it was folded up neatly on the desk right next to the typewriter.

Chloe started to second-guess herself. Didn't she put the sheet on the Royal? She thought she remembered laying the sheet over it before she went downstairs to eat, but did she? She looked at it for a few moments and continued to unconsciously pet Raven's head. She thought that if she hadn't covered it up (but she was sure she did) she certainly did not remember folding that sheet. Even before she lain it over the apparatus, it was not folded; it was just crumpled up in a ball on the floor. That, she was sure of. Had Bill or Sarah been upstairs? She didn't think so. Besides, how would they have gotten past her? She only went downstairs long enough to scarf down a piece of sausage and then she came right back. While she mulled this over in her mind, Raven continued to growl.

"Stop it Raven! There is nothing here for you to be upset about." She tried to scold the dog, but it was hard because she was such a perfectly behaved German Sheppard all the time. She sat at her chair and picked up a Q-tip to continue cleaning the spaces between the keys of the typewriter. She just thought she had to have been the one to remove the sheet. *There was no other explanation, right?* She pondered over this for a few more seconds as she continued to think, *why the hell is it so cold in here?*

Chloe took such care with each key of the keyboard. There was just enough space between them to get her Q-tip all the way down inside and move it around in order to get as much dust as possible out of there. Each letter of the alphabet and each punctuation mark had its own round key which lead it to its corresponding letter or mark inside the Royal. Chloe accidentally pushed the 's' key down when she tried to get underneath it with the Q-tip causing the arm-like structure inside to swing up and slap against the paper roll making a snapping noise which made Chloe jump. She regained herself and giggled before continuing to work.

Other than the subtle noises she made during the cleaning process, the room was quiet. Chloe got up from her chair and went over to her night table where she left her iPod. She searched for a signal for a few minutes, and as soon as she found one, the earbuds went into her ears, launching music from a Pandora radio station straight from the iPod into her brain. She always played her music so loud her father could not believe she hadn't ruptured an eardrum by now. With Metallica's *Master of Puppets* blaring into her ears, she continued to work.

It was Saturday and with Monday being the Labor Day holiday school would be starting on Tuesday, so Chloe knew she only had a couple of days to get her new life in order. She decided to take a break from the typewriter and finish unpacking her belongings so she could get the suitcases out of her room. She had only managed to put about half of her things away the previous night. She had been working on those keys for over an hour and her hand was getting tired. She got up from her chair and carried one of her two suitcases into the closet. She opened it and hung a few black skirts (well, one was purple and black) on the hangers that were already in there followed by some of her shirts, which were also dark colors, and one pair of jeans with holes in the knees and buttock area. Bill didn't like it when she wore those but she really didn't care. Actually, his disapproval only made her where them more.

The second suitcase was filled with leggings, stockings, t-shirts with rock bands on them, one in particular was her favorite because it featured her favorite band, The Pretty Reckless, who she saw in concert last year at the MMRBQ festival in New Jersey. All that was left after that was socks, underwear, a pair of tall black boots, and a pair of black shoes with a slight heel. She only wore those when she was dressed up to go out, which was not very often. The main foot apparel she wore was her black Converse high-top sneakers with the red laces that she wore for the trip to the new house. They matched just about every outfit combination she could come up with from her dismal wardrobe. Besides herself and her dog, they were the most important thing in her life ... although she was getting pretty fond of the Royal she found.

With everything unpacked Chloe decided it was a good time for that walk back to the woods with Raven. She took the sheet and laid it over top of the typewriter and signaled to Raven that it was time. "Want to go for a walk, girl?" Raven knew what that meant and started getting excited and jumped up at Chloe. "Get down, girl. C'mon. Let's go." They walked out the door, down the stairs, and straight out the back door, never even acknowledging the fact they walked right by Bill and Sarah. Chloe put a lot of effort into ignoring them most of the time.

Back in the woods, they found a path which they started to follow. Chloe didn't need to put her dog on a leash because she always stayed right with her. Bill got Raven for Chloe as a companion after her mother died and the two of them had been inseparable ever since. They walked on the path for a while. Leaves and branches fallen from trees cracked under their feet as they made their way deeper into the forest. Chloe wanted to see how far the path went when suddenly she heard a crackling sound to her left that she knew was not from her. She looked and didn't see anyone. She and Raven stopped in their tracks.

"Is someone there?" Just then, she saw him: a young-looking guy with dark hair in a jean jacket was standing about three trees over from her. "Who are you?" she asked as she slowly started to back up.

"I'm Kenneth," the young man said, "but my friends call me Ken. Are you the ones who moved into the old Parrish house?"

"Yeah, I guess. I'm Chloe and this is Raven." She pointed down to her German Sheppard in an attempt to make him aware that she had a large dog with her. Then she retrieved a Marlboro Light package out of her pocket, pulled a cigarette out, and lit it. She thought smoking made her look cool. "We were just going for a walk. I didn't realize anyone else was out here."

Kenneth noticed she was nervous. "I'm sorry if I scared you. I take a walk in these woods just about every day. I live in the one over there." He pointed to the house that was next to Chloe's; however, the houses were pretty spread out. His was one of the yellow Victorians she saw on the way into the neighborhood.

"It's OK. You didn't scare me, not really." She lied as she was taking note of how cute this boy was. "So why aren't you on this path if you are taking a walk?" She took a drag of her smoke and lifted her head to the sky to blow the secondhand smoke away from him in an attempt to be courteous.

"I saw you coming so I hid behind this tree because I didn't want to startle you; however, it appears I have done that anyway so can we just start fresh?" He asked jokingly. "I'm Ken, and you are?"

"Chloe." She blushed as she said her name. *Was*

he flirting with her? She thought he probably was and she didn't mind. She thought he was cute; however, she would never admit that because that would mean she might like him and might be making a friend and friends were something Chloe was not accustomed to.

Kenneth Wright was eighteen years old and attended Hollow Creek High School, which was where Chloe was going to be as of next week. He was also a senior, but he was a year or so older than everyone because he was held back to repeat the first grade. His mom's name was Donna Wright and his father was known as "Sergeant" around the town. He was with the Hollow Creek Police Department. Kenneth had his own car which he bought for himself with money he earned waiting tables at the local Olive Garden. It wasn't a fancy one, just a Honda Civic, but it got him from point A to point B. Unlike Chloe, Kenneth had lots of friends, which she would find out when school started, but for the moment, he was in the woods by himself trying to start a conversation with a young girl he had never seen before. Chloe thought he was strange, but amazing at the same time. Raven sat on the ground next to them, assuming they were going to be talking for a while when Kenneth said, "Do you mind if I walk with you?"

"I was just about to go back to the house." She lied.

"Then I will walk you back to your house. I was getting ready to go home too." He gestured with his hand in a motion to guide Chloe to turn around and head back. Hesitantly, she obliged.

The walk back seemed to be so long due to the fact

Chloe could not find anything to say to this boy. They were both silent as they walked and when they reached the back door to Chloe's house Kenneth asked her, "How is it in there?"

"What do you mean?" She looked confused. "It's OK, I guess."

"Did you know the woman who lived there?" he asked.

"No. Why would I?" She reached for the door handle to go inside.

"I don't know." Kenneth stepped back like he was getting ready to go home. "I just thought maybe that is why you moved into this house, like maybe she left it to your family when she died."

"The woman who lived here died?" Now he got her attention. She knew someone had died here, but now she knew it was the previous owner.

"Yes." Kenneth started talking fast and moved further away. "I mean, yeah. I mean, I have to go. I'll see you soon." He headed to his house in a hurried walk which was closer to a jog.

Chloe went into her house and got a bowl of water for Raven, all the while thinking, *how strange was that?* She thought Kenneth must have been uncomfortable with her appearance. Not a lot of people accepted her Gothic look and she really caked the eye makeup on thick this morning. She did that when she was looking to get a rise out of her dad and Sarah. She knew they did not like it. With Raven happily slurping her water, Chloe opened the refrigerator and pulled out a diet Pepsi for herself. She was so skinny and didn't need to be drinking diet *anything*, but she preferred it over the sugary taste of regular soda. She sat at the kitchen table to drink it. Bill and Sarah must have gone upstairs so she had a moment to herself.

While she sat there and stared at the ceiling she couldn't help but think back to her brief conversation with Kenneth and how he left so nervously. *Was it something I said?* Chloe's mind went back to the moment he told her the previous owner of this house died. Chloe knew her last name was Parrish, but that was the only thing she knew about her except now she also knew about her dying in their house. She did the math. She thought, *Big deal. People die every day.* Chloe thought Kenneth was strange, the way he acted, but that was fine with her because she really didn't care if she ever spoke to him again. It's not like he was her friend or anything. She got up from the table, patted her hip, "C'mon Raven." And the two of them made the long journey back up to their bedroom. She wanted to take a shower before she got any further into this weirdly eventful Saturday.

When Chloe got to her room, she noticed the temperature had not changed in there. She liked the cool temperature, but this was ridiculous. It was supposed to be hot this time of year in Maryland. She also knew Bill had not turned on the air conditioning yet in their new home. She shrugged it off and went straight to her closet to grab the jeans with holes in them and a plain black shirt; actually, it was a blouse with silver buttons from the bottom of it all the way up the neck line. She then got some socks and underwear out of her dresser and turned to walk out of the bedroom when she stopped dead in her tracks. She slowly turned back to look at her desk where Raven was sitting. Once again, the sheet had been removed from the typewriter. The first time it happened she thought that maybe she just forgot to put it over it, but not this time. She knew she had placed that sheet securely around the thing. Someone had to have been in her room. She angrily walked to the top of the stairs.

"BILL?" She hollered down the stairway and only heard her own echo. "BILL?" She tried louder this time.

A voice made it to her which was muffled through the walls. "What is it, Chlo?"

"Who has been in my room?" She asked accusingly. "You guys know you are not allowed in my room!"

Bill appeared at the bottom of the stairs. "Chloe, no one has been up there. Sarah went to the store and I have been down here putting things away." He tried to assure her. "We respect your privacy and have not been in your room, but please don't say we are not allowed up there." Trying to be the disciplinarian, he said, "If I need to go in there for something and you are not around, I *will* go in. Do you understand me? I am still your father; however, this time I have not been in there."

"Whatever." Chloe gave him the spoiled teenager look, narrowed her eyes, and stomped back down her hallway. She just knew he was lying. She gently placed the sheet back in its place and went into the bathroom and got in the shower. With the air being so cold, she had to run the water a little hotter than normal. While she washed her hair, she could not stop thinking about her next move as far as the Royal. She thought she would look at the guts of it next. She rushed through her shower because, suddenly, the only thing she could think of was getting back to fixing that machine.

When Chloe got out of the shower, it was so cold in the bathroom she wrapped a towel around her naked, dripping body, only partially drying herself off, before running back to her room to quickly put on some clothes. She threw the blouse aside and pulled a long-sleeve tee shirt out of her bottom dresser drawer to put on instead. She quickly brushed her hair, not worrying about drying it, and she sat in her chair to face her project.

With the Royal in front of her she looked for the ribbon, which was not hard to find due to it being tangled up with some of the keys. She just wanted to get it out without ripping it so she searched for the spool in order to pull that out first. She had a diagram of what the mechanism should look like displayed on the screen of her laptop in front of her so she could see where the spool should be. Then she hesitated and thought that before she did anything she might want to make sure she would be able to get another one just in case the ribbon broke in the process.

Using her computer, she did a Google search for "Royal typewriter ribbon." She found a little shop called Annie's Odds 'n Ends online and they had what she needed. In fact, they had just about anything you could imagine that had to do with any type of electronic pieces needed to fix most computer-related items. A lot of what the store sold was related to antique machine parts that were used for things most people didn't even own anymore. Everyone was so connected to modern technology. Chloe was surprised they had pieces for a typewriter as old as hers. The only problem was that they were too far away. She would have to order it online and she did not have a credit card. She thought about how she could pull this off and the only scheme she could think of was to steal Bill's credit card. He wouldn't notice. It was only $24.00. She thought about this for a moment and came to the conclusion that if she was going to risk stealing his Visa card, then she had better see if there was anything else she needed for the Royal typewriter so she could order everything at one time.

She looked blankly at the machine for a minute before reaching over to it and grabbing hold of the dust cover. After she removed the dust cover, she could really see inside the machine and noticed that part of the old ribbon looked like it was stuck down inside the body but she couldn't see what it was stuck on. She decided to just pull it out because she figured if it was already a mess it wouldn't matter if it snapped or ripped. She lifted the spool and tugged on the ribbon that was hung up. She tugged and pulled but nothing happened. Getting frustrated she pulled real hard until the ribbon sprung free from the ribbon guide. Chloe's quick reflexes saved the spool from flying across the room as she caught it and held it firmly in her right hand. She squeezed hold of the spool so tight that something on it cut her hand. It appeared to be just a scrape but a couple drops of blood ran down her palm and between her fingers. She jumped, not because it hurt, but because it startled her. She did not have a tissue to clean it up with or to stop the bleeding. She held her right hand up with her left hand in an effort to not let any blood drip onto the floor, but what she didn't realize was that a drop had escaped her, dripped off her wrist and landed right in the middle of the keyboard. It landed between the "G" and "H" keys and caused blood spatter to be planted on the surrounding keys.

"Damn it!" She was pissed. How could one or two drops of blood make such a mess? She got up and quickly went into the bathroom to rinse her hand off with cold water.

In the bathroom, she held her hand under the faucet and let the cold water run over the barely noticeable wound. It stung a little and she looked at it wondering what could have caused the cut in the first place.

When she was all cleaned up she got a damp washcloth out of the bathroom cabinet so she would be able to clean the mess up in her room. She went back to the typewriter and picked up the ribbon spool from the table. There were remnants of her blood on it. That was when she noticed a small piece of metal sticking up out of the center of it. Upon closer inspection, she realized it was just part of the spool that got bent somehow. She thought, *I didn't pull that hard, did I?* She looked at the affected keys and let out a disappointing sigh. How would she clean them? She picked up the dust cover in order to put it back on and noticed she also left blood inside the mechanism between the ribbon vibrator and the platen. She took the washcloth and got to work cleaning up the pieces of her that were embedded in her new toy.

She had to scrub a little but the blood finally came off, except for a smidgen that was underneath the "G" key. She just left that because it was not noticeable unless she actually tilted her head awkwardly to look under the keys. She did not want to cause any more damage so she decided to leave everything else alone for now and just order the ribbon. She quietly went to her dad's bedroom right below hers and found his jeans on his bed. He always left his wallet in his pocket, even after taking his jeans off. She could hear him moving around downstairs so she opened the wallet and snagged the first Visa card she saw and ran back to her room.

Back in her room she immediately got back on her computer where Annie's Odds 'n Ends was still showing on her screen. She clicked on the photo of the black ribbon that matched the one she just removed and clicked "Purchase." The transaction was complete in just a few minutes and Chloe was able to get the Visa card back into Bill's wallet without getting caught. As she started to head back up to her room, there was a knock on the front door of the house. She heard Bill go to the door and open it. There were voices, but she could not make out what they were saying. Then she heard Bill approaching the bottom of the stairs where she stood at the top eavesdropping. She quickly backed away from the stairway so Bill wouldn't see her.

"Chloe?" He hollered in a much softer voice than he normally used when shouting her name. "Chloe? Come down here please."

Peeking down the stairs, she finally responded. "What?"

"There is someone here to see you, says his name is Kenneth."

Chloe thought *what is he doing here?* She took a deep

breath. "I'll be right down." She rushed back to her room, looked in her mirror and rubbed her eyes. This was disastrous! She had not put any make-up on after she got out of the shower. She frantically threw on her signature black eye make-up and some lip gloss. She always put a lot of it on to establish the Goth look that she worked so hard to maintain these days, but there was not time - he was here.

Her hair was another story. It was jet black from the dye she used (she was naturally blonde) and it was still somewhat wet from her shower. She brushed it to smooth it out and threw it back in a ponytail just to get through this encounter. She absolutely did *not* like the ponytail look so she tore the hair tie out of her hair, fluffed her hair with her hands, and let it lay naturally on her shoulders. She decided that would have to do as she turned away from her mirror and headed out of her bedroom, this time leaving Raven behind as she closed the door.

Downstairs in the foyer Bill and Kenneth were having a conversation; well, Bill was having one. Kenneth was just answering the questions that were being fired at him like how was the high school and where did he live... that sort of thing. This caused Chloe to get down the steps quicker to relieve the poor guy of the third degree. She saw him with her dad and went over to them.

Kenneth looked at her. "Hi," he said while kind of nervously looking back at Bill. "Sorry to come over like this."

Chloe looked at Bill with eyes that screamed *GO AWAY!* "It's okay. What's up?" She blushed a little and looked at the floor in an attempt to avoid eye contact with him.

Bill looked at the two of them, knowing they wanted privacy even though they barely knew each other. "Well, I have a newspaper to get back to." He went back into the kitchen which was a relief to Chloe as she was already uncomfortable; she didn't need him hanging around. She also thought for a brief moment that she was glad he was one of the remaining people in the world who still read a newspaper. It gave him a reason to leave. Most people relied on the internet for the latest news anymore.

"I felt like we left things kind of weird earlier today.

Would you like to go for a walk?" Kenneth was so fidgety; Chloe thought it was cute.

"Sure," Chloe said as she glanced back in the direction her father just went. "I have to get out of here for a bit anyway." She opened the door and they went outside.

She immediately fired up a smoke as they started their walk down Honeysuckle Drive. Kenneth pointed to all of the houses along the way and gave her the story of who lived where and for how long, who was worth knowing, and who she should not bother with. He knew everyone in the neighborhood and he was like a tour guide giving background information on everyone. Chloe listened, but she was not really looking at any of the houses he pointed out. She was only really interested in one thing, but wasn't quite sure how to ask so she just interrupted him and blurted out, "What about Mrs. Parrish?"

Kenneth stopped abruptly in his tracks. "Yeah, sorry about that. I should have never said anything." He got so nervous again.

That was not good enough for Chloe. "She died, right? Did she have any family or was she the only one who lived in our house?" She fired the questions at him quicker than he was ready for.

"I'm not sure of everything," he said. Maybe that was true, but the tone in his voice said he knew something. "I'll tell you what I know but not here. Do you want to go back to my house and have a soda or something?"

"Yeah. I'm thirsty anyway. Thanks." Chloe turned around to head back, Kenneth followed.

His house was nice. It was a Victorian just like the Mattson's had just bought and the inside was pretty much the same, with hardwood floors everywhere and a never-ending staircase. They went through the foyer, through the living room, and into the eat-in kitchen where there was a table with six settings of dinnerware laid out and six chairs. It was bigger than her kitchen. The ceiling was high and the cabinets just about reached up to it. Kenneth got two glasses out of one of them and Chloe was glad she didn't have to get her own because she would not have been able to reach them. She thought he must have a large family.

Kenneth noticed her looking around in awe of everything. "It's not as monstrous as it looks. I don't know why my mom insists on this table with all the settings with it just being her, my dad, and myself. It kind of annoys me." He pulled a chair out. "Have a seat. Do you like diet or the real deal?"

"Diet is fine for me." She watched as he got two cans out of the refrigerator, one diet and one regular Pepsi. He even got a bucket of ice out of the freezer. He opened her soda for her and put some tongs into the ice so she could help herself. Once she got her soda cold, she looked at him. "Well? C'mon, tell me about Mrs. Parrish."

Her persistence was unavoidable so he just started

talking, not even sure of what he was saying. "She was in her early sixties, I think, and she lived alone; actually, she lived there a long time and no one ever noticed anyone coming or going out of her house. She was a loner, but they say a lot of writers are."

With this, Chloe stopped him. "She was a writer?"

"Yes. She wrote stories and articles. Every once in a while, we saw one appear in the local paper or in a journal at the bookstore. Why?" He looked at her curious as to why that bit of information seemed to have struck a nerve.

"No reason." Chloe wasn't about to tell anyone about the typewriter she found just yet so she motioned with her hand for him to continue.

"She used to come outside a lot and work in her yard and even take walks down the street. She had a couple of cats that roamed the neighborhood that liked to go to her house because she fed them and gave them milk. I don't know who they belonged to, but she took care of them, for a while anyway." He looked down at the table as if he was searching for something. "After a while, we saw her less often and when she did come outside she was in her bathrobe. That was strange because, even though she was alone, she used to always look nice when she came outside, even to just take the trash out."

Chloe looked up at his face. "Was she sick?"

"I don't think so because her stories kept appearing in the papers and the weird thing was that it was happening more often. It was like she was dropping from the public eye, except for her stories. As a matter of fact, it was when they stopped that people noticed her. That gained the attention of the authorities and they thought something might be wrong with her. One day they finally decided to check on her because a couple of weeks had gone by with no one seeing or hearing from her at all." He looked at Chloe, not sure if he wanted to continue or not. The anxious look on her face told him she was not going to let him stop with this story.

He got up from the table and excused himself in order to use the bathroom. Chloe felt a little uncomfortable sitting alone in his house. She hoped he would be quick and no one would walk in on her. He came back quickly and sat back down. "Do you want some cookies or anything? My mom always has so much junk food around and most of it goes to waste because it's only the three of us. I don't know why she insists on all of this food." He pulled open the pantry door to show her. He could reach it from his seat.

"No, thank you." She honestly just wanted to hear the rest of the story because it was getting real interesting and she knew that he was just trying to stall.

He continued. "One day, the cops went to Mrs. Parrish's house. They banged on the door for a while and when no one answered, they busted the door in. I don't know why cops have to be so dramatic about those things. They probably could have just picked the lock. Anyway, after searching through the house they finally made it up to the third floor where she slept and it was so cold up there. All they found was a nicely polished old typewriter of some sort sitting on her desk in her room, which was spotless. It looked like no one had been living there, but everything was so straightened up and clean. All of Ms. Parrish's belongings appeared to be there, even her purse, which told the officers that she hadn't run off anywhere." Kenneth took a deep breath, looked at her, and continued, "It was as if she just simply vanished. The story around town got out of hand because people were saying she was found dead. The truth is that she was never found at all. Please don't tell anyone about this because I could get in so much trouble for telling you all of this."

"How do you know all of these details?" she asked. "That's a little creepy."

"Like I said, my dad was one of the cops on duty that day. Yeah, that's right. You better behave yourself because you live next door to a cop." He joked in an effort to lighten the mood.

"So that's it?" Chloe asked, "They didn't find anything else?"

"OK. You asked for it." He took a deep breath and continued. "My dad said it was so cold in that room he could see his breath. There was paper in the typewriter and there was one word typed in capital letters. It was the name of someone, a woman I think. I honestly can't remember that part and my dad will not talk about it anymore if I ask him. I've tried."

He waited for a reaction from Chloe. When he didn't get one, he continued, "That part was not in the papers. I only know that because of my father and to tell you the truth, I haven't told anyone else about that. It was about three years ago and that house has been empty ever since. I have always wondered who she was talking about when she wrote that person's name. We never found out if it was a friend, a family member, or just a character in one of her stories." He looked at Chloe whose face was expressionless.

After listening to Kenneth's story, Chloe's head was doing somersaults. It certainly explained a few things, like the typewriter, the chill in her room, and the reason the house was empty for so long. She didn't care; however, she thought it was awesome that an old woman may have died in the room she now lived in. That didn't scare her. In fact, she hoped maybe the old woman's ghost was lingering around. Maybe she would haunt Sarah. She knew that was a crazy thought, but it gave her something fun to think about. They got up from the table and Kenneth walked her home to the house that had suddenly become more interesting. Before leaving her, Kenneth asked, "Hey. How are you getting to school on Tuesday?"

"I don't know. Sarah will take me, I guess." Chloe wasn't happy about that. "She works there, unfortunately."

"Why don't you ride in with me?" He pointed to his car in his driveway. "I'll come over and get you."

"OK." She turned to go inside as he backed away and headed home.

When Chloe got inside, she sat in the kitchen for a few moments mulling over the information she had just received before going upstairs. When she got to her room, she put the old sheet over the typewriter, which had so much more meaning to her now, and decided to put that on hold until the ribbon came in the mail.

Chloe decided she liked the rumors about the old woman dying in her house. It also didn't make sense for Ms. Parrish to just disappear, so something had to happen to her. Either way, there were three things Chloe knew for sure: someone was looking out her window the day they arrived at their new house, it was always entirely too cold in her room, and she was sure someone kept moving the sheet off the typewriter when she knew she had covered it up. Because of all of this, she decided the town rumors were not so far-fetched, but *that*, she would keep to herself.

Tuesday morning came fast and Chloe was not ready for it. She dreaded starting a new school and having to deal with a complete set of new people who would have nothing in common with her, or she with them. The bothersome beeping of her alarm sounded promptly at 6:00 a.m., which would allow her plenty of time to get ready in order to be at her new prison by 7:20am. She let out a morning stretch until every bone and muscle in her body made its debut for the day. Then she went to the closet to pick out what to wear for this day she wished she didn't have to participate in. Along the way, she glanced at her desk where she had left the typewriter covered up with its sheet. Satisfied that it looked undisturbed she continued to her closet door, turned on the light, and grabbed her black leggings with the holes in the thighs. They looked like they had been dipped in a lake full of piranhas. It was a warm morning which she knew would lead to a hot day so she thought her faded cut-off jean shorts would be appropriate attire for the weather. She put those on over top of her leggings, which was another look her father did not approve of. To complete the outfit for her inauguration at Hollow Creek High, she chose a deep, dark red sleeveless t-shirt that was just long enough to meet the top of her shorts.

She went to her dresser where her mirror, makeup,

and manicure items were. She decided her nails looked okay because she had touched up the black polish on them the night before so all she had to worry about was her hair and face.

She looked at herself in the mirror for a few seconds and thought to herself, *Here goes...* She started the process by blotting a pale colored powder foundation all over her face before painting on the darkest gray eye shadow she had; it almost looked black. That was followed up by the thick black eye liner she wore every day. The last thing she had to do for her eyes was the mascara. She had a few of these to choose from, but she chose the darkest black she had in her collection. Chloe wanted the students at the high school to see her and leave her alone. Most of the time that was what people did with her because she went out of her way to look like a corpse and act like she didn't have a care in the world.

She carefully brushed her lashes to boldly cover each one until her look was complete, except she needed something on her lips. Red was the obvious choice; she smoothed it on, blotted her lips with a tissue and she was done with her face. She crunched her hair with a brush to make it look messy and sprayed it with Aqua Net hair spray. Now she was ready for her day of torture and it was just in time because she never heard the knock at the door, but Bill's voice traveled up the stairs. "Chloe. Kenneth's here."

She took one final look in the mirror and headed

out of her bedroom door. Bill would have to let Raven out before he went to work. She didn't have time. "Coming!" she shouted as she started her descent down the stairs.

Ken looked amazingly adorable! He stood by the front door so erect and masculine; Chloe thought that it may have been an attempt to impress her dad. He wore jeans that looked brand new with a black polo shirt tucked into them which made his abs and chest lines visible. His sneakers were black Nikes; Chloe looked down at her Converses with the red laces and compared the two in her mind. He looked like he just stepped out of a catalogue. He looked at her. "Ready?"

Chloe looked over at Bill who was still standing by the door. "Will you let Raven out?" she asked him. "I didn't have time." Assuming he would do as she asked, she walked over to Kenneth. "Yeah, I guess." She said this with the least amount of enthusiasm possible.

Kenneth knew she was probably nervous. He opened the door and they went out to his car; Chloe thought it was silly of him to drive over to get her when he lived right next door, but didn't say anything as he opened the passenger side door so she could get in. He closed the door like a gentleman when she was securely inside, went around the car to get in the driver's seat, and they drove off.

①④

It took only five minutes or so to get to school since they lived so close. Chloe thought the car ride felt a lot longer though because neither one of them spoke the entire time. It wasn't that Chloe didn't have anything to say, it was that she didn't know how to bring up what she wanted to talk about. She wanted more information about Old Lady Parrish, but Kenneth changed the subject so quick the other night so she was certain he did not want to talk about it anymore. At least not yet anyway. Chloe just glared out the window as they pulled in the high school parking lot. Kenneth pulled into a parking space, stepped out of the car, and went around to where Chloe was sitting and opened her door for her.

"Well, this is it!" Kenneth said with a fake voice of excitement.

Chloe looked at him and then at the school, and with a roll of her eyes, she said, "I'm thrilled."

"Yeah, you look it," Kenneth said.

The bell sounded as they walked into the front door of Hollow Creek High School where the halls were filled with students rushing this way and that to get to their classrooms. There were groups of kids gathered around lockers catching up on the events of their summer break. Kenneth walked Chloe to her homeroom; she told him what room she had to find - she received a letter in the mail with that information - and he left her to go start his own day. She thought it was nice of him to drive her to school, but now she was overwhelmed because he was gone and she didn't know any of these other people. She stood in the front of the room trying to decide where to sit when a cheerleader-type blonde walked right into her causing her to stumble into a desk. The girl wasn't watching where she was going because she had her nose imbedded into the face of her cellphone. Chloe narrowed her eyes and looked at her with an intense stare that must have scared the girl because she apologized and sped off to one of the desks in the front row. Chloe went to the back of the room to claim one of those seats before they were all taken. Everyone who came into the room stared at her as if she had a unicorn horn sticking out of her head, but she supposed that was how it was for any new kid in school. Even the teacher couldn't help but stare at her as she called out the students' names and handed out their schedules before dismissing them to go to their first period classes.

Chloe walked down the hall looking at all of the numbers on the classroom doors until she finally found the one she was looking for at the end of the hall. She entered room 155 where she received a completely new set eye balls upon her. She couldn't understand why people felt the need to gawk, so she stared back at them in an attempt to make them feel as uncomfortable as they were making her feel. It appeared to work because one by one, the students turned away from her and talked amongst themselves (most likely about her) until the teacher walked in.

Besides all of the staring from her idiot classmates, the rest of the day went kind of okay until she got to her last class of the day. She was relieved; Biology was the last classroom she had to hunt for that day. The school was huge and Chloe had trouble finding all of her classes because she refused to ask for help. She also hadn't seen Kenneth all day so she figured she would walk home after school since they had not made any plans to meet up after school and ride home together. She certainly was not going to just show up at his car in the school parking lot because she thought that he would think she was putting him on the spot so he wouldn't have a choice but to take her home; not to mention, she didn't want to be rude.

Actually, Rude sat right next to her in Biology with her naturally long blonde hair, which she brushed constantly, and more than enough makeup (not that Chloe should judge) and wearing a white mini dress. Chloe thought if she crossed her legs she would show everything she had underneath it. Her name was Piper Alexander and she was the preppy-type, nose in the air snob who all the other girls wanted to be like. Every school had a Piper Alexander. In her last school it was Shayna McMullen, but Chloe just wanted to forget about her because she could not stand her. This Piper girl sat straight in her seat with her bare legs crossed (and yes, the boys got a peek at her panties) and her hands folded on her desk. Everyone stopped to say hi to her, especially the boys. She looked at Chloe and rolled her eyes from her head to the floor to check her out. The look on her face was one of disapproval and then class started. Even the teacher singled Piper out just to make sure she had a fantastic summer holiday. Class dragged on, partly because it was so boring but mostly because Chloe wanted to get away from the chick who looked and smelled like potpourri.

The final day's bell finally sounded and Piper stopped Chloe as she got up from her desk. "Where you from, new girl?" She said this like Chloe owed her an explanation.

Who was she, the school patrol? Chloe just looked at her in silence.

"I asked you a question!" Piper must have thought she was an authority or something.

Chloe picked up her backpack, flung it over her shoulder, and looked Piper in the eyes. "None of your business." Then she walked out leaving the rude blonde girl speechless standing in the classroom. She walked out of the school and started her journey home on foot.

After she walked about two blocks, Kenneth pulled up behind her. "Going my way?"

She smiled and got in the car. "Thanks."

"How was your first day?" He still looked as fresh as he did that morning.

"It was okay." She lied. She absolutely hated it, but

then again, she hated her last school too. The only difference here was it was new to her.

He could tell by the way she answered him and just stared out of the car window that she did not have the best day. "Aww... it's not so bad once you get to know them."

She thought, *I don't want to get to know them. Screw them!* The rest of the ride was quiet. The radio was not even on. They pulled up the driveway, she thanked him, and started to get out of the car.

"Wait a minute," he said, "Can I drive you tomorrow?" At least *he* was nice. He was the only person who wanted to talk to her, and the only one she cared to talk to. She hoped his niceness wasn't just because they were neighbors because she thought she might be developing a little crush on him. "As I see it, you don't have another option unless you walk or ride with your stepmom, and you've made it perfectly clear you don't care for her."

She knew he was right since she did refused to ride with Sarah. "Yeah, OK." She got out and quickly went into her house where she peeked out the window and watched him drive to his house. She continued to watch as he got out of his car and her eyes followed him straight into his front door.

No one was home yet. Sarah would probably be held up at the school for a while since it was her first day there and Bill wouldn't be home until later. He had a long drive home from work now so Chloe had the house all to herself, which was exactly the way she liked it. She grabbed a soda out of the fridge, let Raven out to pee, and went straight up to her room. She dropped her backpack full of books onto the bed and turned to head back out the door to go to the bathroom. Her bladder was about to explode. She walked toward her desk and froze, putting both hands over her mouth as she gasped. The sheet that was covering up the typewriter looked like it had been thrown on the floor and the blood that she thought she had cleaned off of the keys was there again, all over the keyboard. Only this time, there was more of it. The keyboard was covered with splattered blood. Chloe felt a chill travel through her entire body causing all of her hair to stand on end. *What the hell?* she thought before she said out loud, "I cleaned that shit up!"

She slowly approached the Royal. The cloth she used to clean it sat next to it and it was clean. There was no blood on it and it was folded as if it was never used. Freaked out, she grabbed the towel and threw it over the keys and went to the bathroom. As she sat on the toilet relieving herself, she looked down at her hand which started to ache. The cut in the middle of her palm started to bleed. She got up, wiped herself, and ran the cold water from the faucet in order to wash the blood off her hand. Then she looked in the mirror and said aloud, "What the fuck is going on?"

She dried her hands and went back to her room. She noticed the temperature had dropped from the time she was in there, just a few minutes ago. She looked around frantically and was struck with horror when she saw the typewriter, which was, once again, clean. She knew she had just seen it covered with blood. Then she raised her hands in front of her face only to see that the cut that she knew was there had completely vanished. She ran out of her room, down both flights of stairs, and straight out the front door. Something was very wrong. She ran over to Kenneth's house and pounded on his door.

Kenneth answered the door, which was what she hoped for; she didn't know his parents yet. "Chloe?" He noticed her breathing heavy. "What's wrong?"

"Will you come over my house for a minute?" she asked.

"Sure, just let me turn off the TV." He did that and came back to the door and they went next door.

"It's my room." She didn't really want to bring him up there; she barely knew him, but, at this point, he was all she had. "This way." She led him upstairs.

"You're freaking me out!" he said as Chloe grabbed his hand to pull him faster.

They reached her room and went inside. "There!"

"What? I don't see anything but a typewriter." He was confused.

"You don't feel the cold? Oh, and the typewriter! I cut myself on it. There was blood on it, but the cut on my hand went away." She said as she pointed to where the cut used to be.

"You're not making any sense. Slow down and just tell me what happened." He could tell she was agitated. "And yeah, it's a little chilly in here. It's probably just the air conditioning"

Chloe looked around the room and realized how insane this all must sound to him. He was not going to believe her because he had not seen it. Maybe she *was* going crazy. It could be the move and the start of a new school. She looked at him. "Never mind. I guess I... never mind." She sat on the bed with a look of frustration on her face.

"I'm sorry, Chloe. Do you want to talk about it?"

She shook her head from side to side which told him she did not want to talk about it and then she led him back downstairs. She thought she might just be tired from the long day. She walked him to the front door of her house and he went home looking back at her house before entering the back door of his.

Chloe knew what she saw, but she also knew that trying to explain it to someone else would be impossible. No one else was there and she really did not want Kenneth to think she was crazy because she was starting to really like him.

The next couple of days were uneventful. Chloe's room remained cold but she just covered up with blankets at night and kept to herself about it. There was nothing anyone could do anyway.

Thursday came and so did the anticipated package from Annie's Odds 'n Ends. The box was waiting for Chloe on the front porch when she got home from school. She picked it up and looked at it for a few minutes trying to decide if she still wanted to mess with the typewriter after what happened the other day. She had not touched the Royal since Monday when she had the little episode with Kenneth and nothing else happened that was out of the ordinary; however, she was actually a little scared of it now. She brought the box upstairs and set it down on her desk.

She decided to open the box. She had to cut through the Annie's Odds 'n Ends sticker with a pair of scissors before she could get inside and take the contents out. She put the spool next to the Royal on her desk and came to the conclusion that she had to do as planned and fix the typewriter. She took the ribbon out, put the spool in place, and fed the ribbon through the feeder. Chloe was surprised at how easy it was to install the ribbon, the task being something she had never done before. Then she got out some paper and fed that through so the machine was ready to go. She was impressed with how well she had cleaned the machine and set it up. She turned to get up from her chair when it happened. Her hands moved over to the keyboard and her fingers were placed onto the keys as if she was going to type something. Chloe jumped because she did not move her own hands.

She took a deep breath and got ready to scream, but thought twice about doing that. Then she would have to explain to Sarah what had happened. She wasn't sure if Sarah was home yet, but she was not going to take that chance.

Chloe was suddenly covered from head to toe with goose pimples on top of goose pimples as chills were sent through her entire body. She desperately tried to pull her hands away from the keyboard, but they would not budge. She felt a kind of pressure within her fingertips as the keys started to move. Actually, she was making the keys move; well, her fingers were anyway.

Before she knew it, several of her fingers began plunging downward and she heard the letters striking the paper she had just installed. She looked at her hands and was terrified, so she was not paying attention to the letters her hands were typing.

Suddenly, they stopped. She looked up at the paper and saw the entire ordeal had only produced two words:

Hi Chloe

Chloe was in awe. How did this typewriter know her name? More importantly, what had just happened? Chloe could not take her eyes off the paper as she had no idea how any of this had happened. The only thing she knew for certain was that she, for some reason, was no longer afraid. Actually, she felt some kind of strange comfort inside herself that she could not explain. Something was happening to her; something scary, but wonderful, something that was truly and only hers.

The notion of the house being haunted was suddenly real, or was it? Is this house haunted; and if so, is it Isobel Parrish? So many questions ran through Chloe's head and a crazy thought struck her as she removed her fingers from the keys, which she was easily able to do at that point. She looked at her palms and stretched her fingers out before placing her fingers back on the keys where they were and began to type of her own free will. She wanted to communicate with whoever was doing this so she began to type.

Is someone here with me?

Nothing happened for what seemed like forever (actually it was only about two minutes), but then the Royal began to do something. The keys moved and Chloe's fingers went down with them as each letter pelted the paper.

Y E S

She backed away from the desk and tried to decide what to ask next. If the typewriter could answer her questions, then she had to ask it. As another chill ran through her entire body, she thought for a moment before proceeding back to the keys. She started asking questions as if she were playing with a Ouija board; however, she was just alone with the typewriter in her bedroom.

Who are you?
Are you Mrs. Parrish?

She stopped there and waited for a response. Nothing happened. She thought she was going crazy. She repeated the questions and after waiting for what seemed like an eternity for an answer, she got up from her seat and went downstairs to get a Diet Pepsi with her questions unanswered. When she returned to her room, there had still been no response from whomever or whatever she was talking to.

Frustrated and confused, Chloe pulled the paper out of the machine, crumpled it up, and threw it in her trashcan. She covered the machine up and sat on her bed to do homework to try to forget about the events that just took place. She had some calculus and some English homework. For English, they had to write an essay on who their favorite literary author was from the nineteenth century and why. This would be easy for her because she was a loner who did a lot of reading, and what she read was usually of the horror genre so the obvious choice for her from that era was Edgar Allan Poe. They also had to write a short story of about 500-1000 words which, they felt, could be compared to a work by their chosen author. She had three days to complete both the story and the essay so she started with the fact-based essay on Poe.

For an hour, she labored away on her laptop, typing the many qualities she loved about Poe's work: it had a creepy voice, his characters, who were mostly insane, and the melancholy structure of his works were horrifyingly wonderful. When she was finished her essay of 542 words, she saved her file and started a new one for her short story. She was going to write about a murder since a lot of those happened upon Poe's pages. She started to type and before she got the opening sentence completed the screen on her laptop went black. She thought it was the battery so she got the cord and plugged it in. Nothing. She looked over at the old typewriter on her desk and debated in her head whether or not to use it. She wanted to get the assignment done and did not want to take the time to figure out what was wrong with her computer because she still had the calculus assignment to do as well.

Her favorite story by Edgar Allan Poe was "The Tell Tale Heart." She thought she would mirror that a little by placing her main character in an insane asylum and killing someone. She was just pissed because the story would take her longer to type on the fossil in front of her than it would have on her laptop. She began to plug away at the story. She placed her main character in the psych ward over at the main hospital where she escaped from her bed after pretending to take her medicine. She named her Nancy and, Nancy had been hiding all of her pills under her mattress every day. Chloe knew this part was kind of cliché due to all of the patients in the movies doing this same thing, but she didn't care. It worked for her story. Nancy put all of the pills in the pocket of her robe, went down the hall to the nurse's station (unnoticed of course) and put all of the pills in a freshly brewed pot of coffee. She figured they would dissolve in there. She then made it back to her bed (again, unnoticed). When her nurse came in her room later that night to check Nancy's vitals, she stumbled and collapsed after pumping up the blood pressure cuff she had just placed on Nancy's arm. The pills worked and Nancy got out of bed again, strangled the nurse, and made her way down the hall to where the other two nurses were slouched over the desk, obviously knocked out also. Nancy stabbed each one of them in the throat with a pen because that was all she could get her hands on at the desk.

With all three nurses dead, Nancy felt a horrible sense of paranoia that she would get caught so she left the hospital and walked straight to the police station and turned herself in. That was it; the villain committed murder and felt guilty and paranoid, just like in "The Tell Tale Heart." Chloe knew it was a cheesy story, but the assignment was done and she turned it in to her teacher the next day to get it in early.

A week went by and Chloe was settling into her new routine, which was pretty much the same routine she had at the last place; school sucked, the teachers sucked, the students sucked (except for Ken of course), and she had developed a new form of dealing with her stepmom. She ignored her, even more than she had before. Bill was never home from work until about 8:00 p.m. so Chloe hung out with Ken a lot. They had become pretty close in just a short amount of time. He took her to school and brought her home every day and they hung out after they were done their homework. Well, Chloe didn't do hers half the time, but Ken was a stickler for getting his done and he usually helped Chloe a little with hers whether she wanted to do it or not.

Ken was at her house one evening when her dad had just gotten home from work. Bill sat down and turned on the evening news. Sarah brought his dinner to him in the living room so he could enjoy a little television while he ate. Chloe and Ken could hear the TV because Bill always had it turned up so loud so he could hear it if he were to leave the room. The reporter's voice was distracting Chloe so she asked if Ken wanted to go upstairs to finish their work because it would be less noisy up there.

They got up from the table and walked through the

living room (Bill didn't even notice them) and Chloe glanced over toward the television where a bleached blonde woman with bright red lipstick who was wearing a red blouse that was entirely too tight was doing a live report from the local hospital. There were police cars all around her and people running in and out of the hospital doors while the police tried to unroll the yellow police tape that would eventually keep everyone out. Chloe stopped to listen to the report and was astounded when she heard that a patient killed a couple of people inside the ER before fleeing the scene on foot. Chloe froze and dropped the book she was holding as Ms. Bleach Blonde Reporter said, "It is believed that the patient stabbed the two women and fled on foot. We are not releasing any names at this time so the families can be notified."

Chloe picked up her book and continued with Ken upstairs, completely distracted now with her mind racing. Chloe started thinking the worst. She knew that story. The victims were probably nurses and the patient would probably be turning herself in so the job of law enforcement would be easy. Chloe knew the story because she had just written it! She didn't say anything to Ken about it because she knew he would just think she was jumping to conclusions over nothing. He would think it was just a coincidence. *Hell, maybe it was.*

They finished their homework and Kenneth went home. Chloe never mentioned the news report or the similar story she had written. She just let him leave, hoping the subject would never come up.

17

Later that Sunday evening, Mrs. Wright was cooking dinner when Chloe came to the door. The aroma of lasagna, which had been baking in the oven, consumed Chloe's senses as she entered the house at the welcoming hand of Mrs. Wright, who was getting used to Chloe coming over to hang out with her son. She told Chloe she could go on up to Ken's room where he was listening to music and studying. Chloe could here ACDC's *Back in Black* emanating through the floor boards. He also liked his music loud and listened to hard rock - one of the reason's she liked him so much. She knocked on his door and he opened it, looking surprised to see her.

"Hey Clo. Sorry ... let me turn that down."

"No," she said. "I love this shit and Sarah is getting on my nerves!" She pushed past him and plopped down onto his bed. "I need to blow off some steam!" The fact was that she and Sarah had barely crossed paths that day, but for some reason, she felt like she needed justification for stopping by unannounced like this, even though she did it all the time.

He went over and sat next to her. He put his hand on her knee, which surprised them both, and then quickly pulled it away. They were not a couple or anything, although, at times, it seemed like they were. She looked at him through her mounds of black eye liner with eyes that looked as depressing as the makeup that surrounded them. She was in need of someone to understand her and she felt like she never got that at home. She cupped his hand with hers and gently laid it back in place on her knee. He looked into her eyes with almost the same expression she had in her eyes. Neither one of them spoke as their eyes locked.

Kenneth's lips lowered slowly to meet hers. He planted a soft, moist kiss on her partially opened lips before allowing his tongue to enter her mouth to massage hers. They engaged in an erotic French kiss before he leaned her slowly back onto his bed. He caressed the side of her face with one of his hands and placed the other on her hip. She had a miniskirt on which made it easy for his hand to find its way up her thigh.

He stopped for a moment to get up to lock his bedroom door, and before he had returned to his bed, Chloe moved her legs up onto the bed and cocked her head slightly to look at him with her black stare, the one that freaked everyone out except Kenneth. He quickly came back to the bed, unzipped his jeans, and climbed on top of her. She showed her approval with her heavy, hot breath in his ear. His hand quickly found its way to her thigh and he grabbed a hold of her panties and slid them down her legs. She kicked her sneakers off to make it easier for the panties to come off. He dropped them on the floor and moved his hands to his own jeans where Chloe's hands were already attempting to slide them down over his hips.

She felt his hardness through his boxers and squeezed his body closer to hers. He pulled his boxers down with one hand while she undid the buttons on her blouse one by one. His throbbing penis slid into her and she let out a small moan. He silenced her by wrapping his lips around her mouth and violently kissing her as he penetrated her. They had amorous juvenile sex for only a few minutes before he ejaculated into her. She felt him pulsating deep inside her as he let out every ounce of semen he had into her before collapsing his entire body on top of hers.

It was the best sexual experience she had ever had, not having much to compare it to. They lain there in silence breathing heavily for a few minutes before he pushed himself off of her. He stepped off the bed and looked at her, not knowing what to say. She buttoned her blouse closed, sat up, and swung her legs off the side of the bed. After gathering her panties off the floor and getting herself back together, she stood up and kissed him on the cheek to let him know that what they had just done was okay.

"Kenneth?" They both jumped when they heard Mrs. Wright's voice holler from the bottom of the steps. "Dinner is ready."

"Do you think she heard us?" Chloe asked him.

"I doubt it. We were pretty quiet," he said as he took her hand in his. "Are you okay? I'm sorry, Chlo. I didn't mean for that to happen."

"Don't worry about me. I'm fine, and yes, I think we

both meant for that to happen," she said. "Don't worry about anything. I am on the pill."

She knew he was thinking that but probably was afraid to say anything because he let out a sigh of relief. They had only known each other a couple of weeks and weren't even dating but that wasn't Chloe's style. The dating thing, that is. At her old school, even though she had only had sex a few times and only with two guys: one in tenth grade when she lost her virginity and one in eleventh which was only a bet for that guy and she was called a slut and a whore by most of the girls there. It was a reputation she did not deny because it kept people away from her and she liked her seclusion.

"Well, I have to go anyway," she said. "You have to eat. Will I see you tomorrow?"

"Yeah. Aren't I taking you to school?"

"Oh, I guess so. You don't have to if you don't want." She felt bad about what had happened; well, she felt like *he* felt guilty and that was *not* how she wanted him to feel.

"I'll pick you up in the morning. Call me if you need me." He sounded sincere. "I have to go down and eat, but Chloe, are you sure you're alright?"

"Yeah. I just came over because Sarah was working my nerves as usual." She turned and walked out of his room leaving him standing there not knowing what else to say. It turned out, he did feel guilty about having sex with her. He just was not going to tell her that.

The next morning, Ken picked Chloe up for school.

It was the start of a new school week and the car ride was quiet as usual. He had music on but neither one of them said anything, which made it uncomfortable for both of them. They got to school, went their separate ways, and she didn't see him again until lunchtime, but he hung out with some guys and didn't see her.

Chloe made herself scarce that day, except for Piper. She wasn't too bad on most days, or at least it wasn't anything Chloe could not handle, but this particular day started off with Piper pushing past Chloe in the hallway, obviously rushing to class, and knocking her books out of her hands. Piper turned to look at Chloe in the middle of the hall with her things scattered all over the floor, but did not offer her any help. She just kept going. Chloe picked up her books and tried to get on with her day. The bell rang between second and third period and Chloe was leaving English to head to gym class. Piper was in her path with her stuck up friends giggling and walking like they all had something stuck up their asses. The clan was headed her way with Piper leading the pack. When they got to where Chloe was standing by her locker, the attempt was made to knock Chloe's books out of her hands again, only this time it didn't go quite as Piper had planned. Chloe turned toward her and dropped her books on her own.

"What the fuck is your problem, bitch?" She barked at Piper. The other three girls just stood there and said nothing.

Piper was surprised, "Nothing. I didn't see you." She

lied as she giggled that fake laugh that all the blonde Barbie-types in school had.

"Bullshit! You have had a problem with me since the first day of school." Chloe was pissed. She looked straight into Piper's eyes and pushed her backwards a couple of steps. "Back the fuck off, Piper!" Then she walked off to class leaving a hallway full of shocked teenagers behind. She was in a bad mood and didn't have time for anyone today, most of all, Piper Alexander.

The rest of the day was okay until she was leaving her last class. Chloe exited the school and Piper was on the stairs talking with some people. Chloe tried to just walk down the steps and ignore her until she walked right past her and heard someone say, "Bitch." It was soft but she knew it was Piper. She immediately turned to her and grabbed her arm to pull her off the steps.

"Let go of me, you psycho!" Piper yelled and before the girls knew it they were surrounded by the entire student body it seemed.

"You have a problem with me? Let's solve it! Right now, bitch!" Piper backed away but Chloe followed with one step and punched her in the cheek. Shouts and cheers came from all directions; it was mostly the kids rooting for Piper to kick Chloe's ass.

Piper jumped on Chloe and starting smacking her and pulling her hair until they both fell to the ground. Chloe was able to get one more slug in before Mr. Murphy, the eleventh-grade gym teacher, broke the girls apart and made the spectators leave. It was the end of the school day so he could not send them to the principal's office so he told them to meet there first thing in the morning. He would be there also to make sure they showed up. Both of them agreed and Chloe looked around to see if Kenneth was anywhere outside. She didn't see him so she walked to the place he parked his car that morning. The car was there but he wasn't, so she leaned up against it and waited for him. He showed up a few minutes later and they got into the car. Chloe's hair was all messed up and her eyes looked like she had been crying because she was so mad. He looked over at her and put his hand on her knee. She just looked down at the floor.

"Can we just go home?" she asked.

"Everything okay?" He knew it wasn't, but he had to ask. He obviously did not see or hear about the fight.

She looked at him. "I hate this fucking school!" she shouted. She was angry, partly because of the fight with Piper but also because she and Kenneth had sex and he hadn't really spoken to her since then. "Just take me home!"

He did and, once again, the ride was quiet.

At home, before she could get out of the car, he grabbed her hand. "Wait a minute. Can we talk?"

"What about?" She knew damn well what it was about. She just wanted to hear him say it.

"About yesterday. Chloe, I have not been able to stop thinking about it, and you," he said.

"What? Do you want another quickie or something?" She snapped at him.

He got defensive right back at her. "What is your problem? I'm sorry I've been quiet. I just haven't known what to say. I feel like, well, I don't know how I feel. I just feel like we should talk about it."

"What is there to talk about?" she asked as she tried to break free of his grasp.

He pulled her back. "Nothing." Then he planted a kiss right on her lips, which caught her off guard, but she willingly kissed him back. When they broke free from each other, Chloe sat back in her seat and started to cry.

"I'm sorry," he said. "I just care about you."

She looked at him, wiping her eyes. "I care about you too; I'm just not sure how to handle this. No guy has ever cared about me before." Her face was streaked with black makeup as she tried to wipe away her tears.

"Maybe you haven't let anyone, Chlo. Honestly, I don't know what it is but I never felt this way." He was sincere. "Do you want to go out for a bite to eat or something tonight?" As he waited for an answer, he opened the glove compartment of the car and handed her a tissue out of it.

"Sure," she said and then got out of the car. She leaned back in the passenger window and said, "I'll come over after I let my dog out."

She went home where Raven anxiously greeted her at the door. She gave her dog a hug and let her outside.

She felt happy for the first time since they moved here. She had just had a horrible day, but Kenneth just made it better for her and she knew things would be okay, for now.

Upstairs in her room, Chloe was getting ready to go out with Ken. She had to pick out the perfect outfit. *Was this a date?* She was not sure. She changed her clothes and went into her bathroom to wash her face where her makeup had stained her cheeks. She brushed her hair and started to put a fresh coat of makeup on when she heard someone downstairs. It was Sarah. She could hear her talking on the phone to someone. She tried to quietly go downstairs to leave for Ken's house unnoticed, but Sarah stopped her and asked, "What happened today?"

"Nothing," Chloe said as she tried to go out the door.

"Chloe. I work at the school. I heard about your little disagreement today." She was calm and just trying to talk with her stepdaughter, but Chloe didn't want to hear it.

"It was nothing!" Chloe snapped at her, walked out the door, and slammed it shut. Then she quickly walked over to Kenneth's house before Sarah could react to stop her.

Mrs. Wright answered the door and told Chloe that Ken would be right down. Then she went back to a news show she was watching on television. Chloe stood in the living room nervously waiting for Kenneth when something on the news caught her eye. She recognized the reporter on the television from her last report of that hospital patient who killed a couple of people. Once again, she was talking about that same story. Apparently, the authorities had more details regarding the case. The patient was female and the people she killed *were* nurses. The patient then turned herself in. It was exactly the scenario that Chloe wrote about on that typewriter. She was frozen in front of the television until Kenneth tapped her on the shoulder.

"You ready?" He asked.

She just looked at him and nodded, not knowing whether or not she should mention the news broadcast to him. They went out the front door and walked to his car. He took her to the Olive Garden where he worked as a server so he could introduce her to a few people. He thought it might help get her out of her shell a little bit. He introduced her to the few people who came over to their table while they ate and she nodded and shook hands with them to be polite, but she could not get that story she saw on the news out of her head.

When they were finished eating, Chloe decided to just have him take her home where she gave him a quick kiss on the cheek and went inside. There was no way she was going to tell him about that. How could she? What would she say? How would she even bring it up? All of these questions flooded her head as she entered the front door of her house.

Bill and Sarah were talking in the kitchen. Sarah

filled Bill in on the events of the day and, of course, she made Chloe sound like the bad person in the whole thing. Chloe tried to defend herself with her father, but he just shrugged it off and told her to just try to keep her nose clean. He was used to her being an outcast so he assumed it was her fault anyway.

After an argument that lasted about ten minutes between the three of them, Chloe stormed out of the kitchen, got Raven, and stomped upstairs to her room, all the while thinking about the reporter and the news story from earlier that day. She went over to her desk and ran her fingers along the top of the keyboard of the Royal and thought, *Is it possible? Do I have ESP or something?* Just then Raven started to growl. She was staring at the typewriter again.

"What's the matter girl?" Chloe asked her dog. "It's okay. There's nothing there."

Chloe sat at her desk chair and started to pet Raven's head to calm her. One of the keys of the Royal snapped down and typed on its own. Chloe jumped and looked at the paper which was loaded into the machine and saw a single "P" typed on the paper. Confused, she asked herself aloud, "What the hell?" Then the typewriter continued on its own to spell one word:

PIPER

19

The next day was Tuesday and Chloe tried to push what happened with the typewriter out of her head on her ride to school with Kenneth. She just told him she was tired and didn't feel like talking. The silent car rides were becoming an almost daily thing.

Chloe and Piper showed up at the same time at the principal's office that morning. They glared at each other with narrowed eyes before Mr. Netzkey, the principal, showed up and only gave them a slap on the wrist with his threat: if anything like that fight happened again, they would both get a week's worth of detention, and they could possibly be suspended. Of course, Mr. Netzkey seemed to single Chloe out by making it seem like she was the one who was having trouble adjusting to a new school and she was going to have to abide by the way they did things.

"I don't know what you got away with at your last school, Miss Mattson, but we will not tolerate that kind of behavior here," he said in an authoritative voice.

Chloe didn't say a word. *Whatever*, she thought. She was used to being blamed for everything. Why should this school be any different than the last one?

She attended her morning classes that day and did not have her homework assignments for two of them, not only because she had gone out with Ken last night and didn't give herself any time for homework, but also because she could not bring herself to sit and work on the typewriter that had a mind of its own last night. Her laptop was still not working, which was weird because the thing was new and it worked fine before they moved to Hollow Creek.

The day was almost over and Chloe was headed to her last class of the day when she walked past Piper and her Barbie doll friends. Everything had been fine all day but, again, Piper just had to say something. Chloe heard her mumble to her friends: "Where does she buy her clothes, the circus?" They all laughed in that annoying, giddy, girly giggle the way those valley girl types always had.

Chloe turned back toward them and just gave them an evil glare out of her midnight black eyes. That did not seem to faze the girls because they proceeded to walk her way toward the stairs that lead to the first floor where Chloe's last class was located. Chloe started down the steps in an attempt to ignore them, but the girls followed.

She did not see what happened, but heard the screams loud and clear. Chloe heard Piper's ear-piercing scream as she tumbled down the stairs. She rolled right past Chloe and a few other students who were on the steps, hitting every step on the way down; her legs and arms flailed violently in every direction. Her books flew everywhere as some students tried to come to her aid, but it was impossible because they also would have fallen if they got too close to the catastrophe that was taking place. The sounds of screams and books hitting the tiled steps echoed in the stairwell and down the hall before Piper's mangled body came to a rest at the foot of the stairs. The entire episode seemed to happen in slow motion and take several minutes, but in reality, it was only seconds. Some people just stared at Piper on the floor, while others ran to try to help her. She wasn't moving, so no one moved her for fear of hurting her worse.

Not knowing what to do, Chloe ran down the steps to see if Piper was okay and another student ran and got the nearest teacher out of her classroom to help. Piper's nose was bleeding, one of her legs looked severely broken because it was bent in an unnatural way. She was breathing quick, shallow breaths. Mrs. Grande, who had just come out of her history class – and now those students were plastered up against the window trying to see what was going on - got her cell phone out of her pocket and called 911. When the ambulance was on its way, she asked the students what happened but no one knew anything. No one saw what happened. She asked Chloe directly because everyone knew about their fight yesterday.

"I don't know. Maybe she tripped, but I didn't see what happened." Chloe did not look at the teacher when she spoke because she knew what Mrs. Grande was probably thinking.

Of course the Barbie dolls were all crying dramatically because their leader was unconscious on the floor. Lord knew what they would say when they finally got it together enough to be asked what happened.

Two paramedics came rushing down the hall with a stretcher and everyone jumped out of their way as Mrs. Grande tried to get everyone to go to class. Her efforts went unanswered as everyone stayed put because they did not want to miss anything. Mr. Netzkey showed up behind Chloe and he was talking on the phone to Piper's mom about the incident. He told her to just go to the hospital and he would meet them over there when he got things under control at the school.

The paramedics checked Piper's vital signs before strapping her onto the stretcher. Then they went back down the hall with her and loaded her into the back of the ambulance. In no time, they were racing down the road, lights and sirens screaming. It was just about the end of the school day so when the excitement was all over a few teachers cleared the hall of students and sent them home. Chloe didn't realize Kenneth was standing on the steps. She went over to him, took his hand, and they walked out to his car, not saying a word.

Kenneth opened the car door for her and she got in the passenger side of his car. "You alright, Chlo?"

"I'm fine." She just looked down at her lap.

"What happened?" He asked.

Chloe got defensive and looked at him, "I don't know. I guess she just tripped. I had nothing to do with it!" Her voice was harsh and sounded angry.

"I didn't say you did. Calm down. I just thought you might have seen something. That's all."

"Well, by the way everyone was acting toward me, I could tell they all thought I pushed her." Chloe started to sound paranoid. "I didn't. She was behind me and came flying past me. She's just a stupid klutz!"

Kenneth started the car. "OK. We don't have to talk about it anymore." He drove her home and didn't say another word about it.

Before Chloe got out of the car, she turned to him and said, "I need to tell you something." She hesitated, but then opened the door and said, "Never mind." She slammed the car door shut, ran up to her house, and was in her front door before he had time to react.

He just sat in her driveway for a few seconds and looked at her house in confusion before driving home. She went straight up to her room and threw herself onto her bed and started to cry. She didn't even know why. Then she sat up and kicked her legs over the side of her bed, sitting in such a way that her desk with her typewriter was in her view. The paper was still in it with that single word typed on it.

P I P E R

She ran across the room, grabbed hold of the paper, and yanked it out of the platen. Then she tore it into a bunch of little pieces and threw it into her trashcan. That's when she heard voices downstairs. It was Sarah and Bill. She figured Sarah must have called her father and asked him to come home early. She opened her bedroom door in an attempt to hear what they were saying.

"The students said she just fell," Bill said to Sarah.

She responded, "She may have, but her friends are telling a different story."

Chloe knew what that meant. They were lying, saying that she pushed her. She just knew it. She was nowhere near Piper. Chloe thought it would be just like Sarah to blame her for something she didn't do. Chloe could not stand her. She went to the top of the steps where she could hear the conversation better. They spoke some words back and forth and as far as Chloe could make out Bill was not sticking up for her either. He was just agreeing with Sarah the way he always did to try to avoid confrontation with her. Then the phone rang. Chloe only heard Sarah's side of the conversation and was debating in her mind, whether or not to go downstairs. After a couple of sighs, she said. "Please keep me posted." She hung up the phone and started talking to Bill again.

"That was Mrs. Grande," Sarah said.

"What did she say?" asked Bill. "Is Piper okay?" His voice got softer and Chloe figured it was because they knew she was home and didn't want her to hear them.

"What is it, Sarah?"

"Will you call you daughter down here?" she asked. "I think she should hear this and I know she is upstairs."

Bill went to the bottom of the steps. "Chloe? Are you up there?"

She was quiet for a moment and then finally answered. "Yeah! I'm doing homework!" She lied.

"Will you come down here, please?" he asked and then he heard her footsteps coming toward the stairway where he was standing. When she appeared at the top of the stairs, he asked, "Will you come down? We have something to talk with you about."

She didn't say anything. She just started coming down the steps one at a time in a turtle's pace. She was in no hurry to hear whatever it was they had to tell her. She knew it was about Piper and she knew she would be blamed for something.

Chloe met her father at the bottom of the steps and they walked into the kitchen together where Sarah was waiting for them. "Hi, Chloe." she said. "Will you sit please?"

"No. I'd rather stand."

"OK." Sarah knew from experience it was not worth the argument with Chloe because she would surely lose. "I just got a call from Mrs. Grande. She rode in the ambulance to the hospital today with Piper." Sarah waited for a response from Chloe and when she didn't get one, she continued. "Piper is in ICU in critical condition."

Chloe just looked at the floor without saying anything. Her eyes filled with tears and she didn't want anyone to see that.

"At this point, she is still unconscious and they say she should come out of it, but they won't know exactly how badly she is hurt until she wakes up." Sarah looked at Bill, "Will you help me here?"

Bill took the hint. "Chlo, they said she fractured her spine in three places."

That got Chloe's attention because she looked up at them. "Is she going to be okay?" Chloe cried. "What does that mean?"

Her dad tried to partially hug her, but she pulled away. "They said she probably won't be able to walk."

"What?" Chloe's cries intensified. "What do you mean?"

"She broke her back, Chloe." He repeated for clarification. "She has no function from her chest down to her feet." He looked right into Chloe's eyes. "They won't know how bad her head injury is until she wakes up."

Bill barely got that last sentence out before Chloe ran out the back door slamming it behind her. She ran straight over to Kenneth's house and started pounding on his back door. His parents were not home, luckily. She beat and door with her fists repeatedly until Kenneth finally appeared and saw she was crying hysterically.

When he finally got the door open, she ran right past him to get in. He looked outside to see if anyone followed her (like her dad) but there was no one so he closed the door and went to her. She ran into the living room and sat on the couch.

"What is it, Chlo?" he asked.

"She's paralyzed! She's paralyzed and her head is hurt!" Chloe cried and she could barely catch her breath.

"What do you mean?"

"Piper!" she screamed. "She might never walk again and she might be brain damaged!" She screamed at him as if it was his fault.

"Calm down! How do you know?" He asked.

"They called Sarah and told her so my dad told me!" She was looking down at the floor. "What am I gonna do?"

"What do you mean, what are you gonna do?" He was confused. "Is there something you're not telling me?"

"No!" She snapped. "Never mind!"

"Chloe, what is going on? You keep doing that!" He knew she was hiding something. "Just tell me. What's the matter?"

She looked up at him as tears leaked out of her eyes leaving streaks of black makeup down her cheeks. "Nothing. You will think I'm crazy. Maybe I am going crazy." She was a little calmer. Then she stood up. "I have to go." And she walked out.

Kenneth tried to stop her and followed her out the back door, but she yelled at him to stay away from her. Defeated, he went back into his house and tried to call her on her cell phone, but she didn't answer. He tried four times before giving up.

When she got back to her house, she went straight up to her room as usual. She ran up the steps and when she got to her room she slammed the door shut. Her parents were used to that.

She plopped down on her bed, lied back on her pillow, and started sobbing. She felt like the entire world hated her, which usually didn't bother her, but this time, they were wrong. She had nothing to do with Piper's fall and she knew that everyone would think differently because of their fight the other day. She cried for a few minutes and then got up to go to the bathroom.

She walked past the typewriter, which was still sitting on the desk with no paper in it because she had ripped it out, and threw the sheet over it. She didn't want to have anything to do with it anymore.

In the bathroom, she took a much-needed piss and cleaned up her face the best she could. Then she got a glass of water and brought it back to her room. When she got back to her room she stopped in her tracks and dropped the glass of water. It went crashing to the hardwood floor and shattered into dozens of pieces. She put her hands over her mouth as to not scream at what she was looking at. The typewriter was uncovered, there was paper loaded into it, and there was one word written on it; only this time the word was repeated hundreds of times and covered the entire sheet of paper:

PIPER PIPER PIPER PIPER PIPER

Her name was on the paper again, but this time it was written over and over again with no spaces in between. Chloe ran out of the room leaving the glass all over the floor. She ran outside just to get out of the house. She thought she might run over and finally tell Kenneth what was going on, but she stopped in her yard and thought that might not be a good idea. The last couple of times she saw him she was preoccupied by things that kept happening and she was worried he was probably mad at her because of the way she had left his house earlier that day. Then she decided that was a chance she would have to take because she had to tell someone and he was her only friend.

Chloe sat on the grass in her front yard trying to decide what to do. She had her cell phone, which displayed four missed calls from Kenneth. She pondered over what to do. She could call Ken and have him come outside. *No!* She couldn't do that. What would she say? She went back and forth with this in her mind for a little while until she saw Mrs. Wright pull up in the driveway next door. She was just getting home from her part-time job in a small bookstore. Hollow Creek Books was one of those privately owned little businesses which would eventually go out of business because there was talk of a Barnes & Noble opening up on the main highway in town by Christmas. Although Mrs. Wright loved her job - she was the one who read stories to the little kids on Saturday mornings - she didn't really need the money. Her husband had been on the police force for most of his working career and was making a pretty penny.

As Chloe watched her go into the house, she wished none of this was happening. She has always been the one who was not afraid of anything and would welcome a ghost in her own home, which is why she liked the idea of possibly having their new home haunted. Well, now that everything happened with the Royal and Piper, her perspective was changing. She didn't know what to think. Mrs. Wright was inside the house and Chloe looked at her cell phone for a minute. Then she finally got up the nerve to call. Kenneth answered on the first ring like he had been waiting for her call.

"Hello?" he asked, even though he knew it was her.

"Can you come outside?" Chloe asked. "I have something to talk to you about and I know your mom's home so please just come out."

He could tell she was upset. "Alright. Give me a sec." Then he hung up.

Chloe was nervous. What would he say? She didn't want to think too much about how crazy this all would sound to him because she knew she would talk herself out of telling him. The door to his house opened and he walked out, causing Chloe's stomach to plummet. She was petrified and he was headed her way. Her hands were fidgeting. She was still sitting on the ground. She didn't stand up until he got right next to her.

"Chlo, what's going on?" he asked as he helped her up off the ground. "You're acting weird and it's scaring me."

"I don't know," she cried. "Everything...today...Piper's hurt! She's really hurt! They called my house."

"Slow down! You're not making any sense. You already told me they called your house." He tried to calm her down. "Did they call again with more news?"

"No. I'm just so confused I can't remember what I told you." Chloe was sobbing. "What am I gonna do?"

"Wait! What?" He was confused. "What do you mean, what are you going to do? You didn't have anything to do with this, right?"

She screamed. "NO! Of course not, but I think they think I did." She grabbed his hand hard. "Come with me."

"Chloe, what are you doing?"

"Just come with me, Ken!" She pulled him all the way to her house and into her back door before dragging him past Bill and Sarah without even looking at them. She pulled him upstairs to her bedroom where the door was closed. She wrapped her hand around the knob like she was going to open it, but hesitated and looked back at him. "I'm sorry. I just don't want you to think I am crazy." Then she opened the door and took him inside.

The glass was still on the floor from the glass she dropped and there was water everywhere. Ken just looked around, trying not to step on any of it. "What happened in here?" He carefully tiptoed through the mess to get to her bed and sat down.

"See that typewriter over there? I found it when we moved in and I fixed it. Now it works again." She looked at it surprised because the paper that was in it was gone. "No! No!" She went over to it. "There was paper in it, Ken! I swear!" she pleaded. "It had Piper's name on it."

"What the hell are you talking about?"

"I didn't do it! Piper's name was typed on this stupid typewriter and I didn't fucking do it!" She got more anxious.

"Chloe, you need to slow down and tell me what the hell you are talking about."

"The typewriter. It's like it knows stuff." She looked at him to try to read his face. "It knew something was going to happen."

"What?"

"Aren't you listening to me?" She yelled at him. "It typed her name and then she fell! And there was another thing."

"What?"

"I didn't think anything of it, but you know that story I had to write for school? You know, the night I couldn't come out with you? Well, the story I typed on this stupid machine, sort of came true!" She was crying again.

"What story?" he asked. "Chlo, I don't know what's going on but there's nothing here." He said as he also pointed to the desk. "Are you alright?"

"No! I'm not alright!" she screamed. "I want this

thing out of here. Can you at least help me move it?"

"Sure. Where do you want it?" He asked.

She pointed to her closet where it came from in the wooden crate in the corner. "It was in there when I found it. I want it back in there and it is too heavy to move on my own."

"OK. I will move it." He tried to pick it up and then he realized how heavy it was. "It's real heavy. Can I just drop it in when I get it over there?"

"Yeah. I don't freaking care. Just get it out of my room!"

He picked up the typewriter and made a grunting sound because of the weight. He walked it over to where Chloe was. The weight of it was pulling him down so much he was crouching while he walked. When he got to the wooden box, he dropped it in like he said he would. It appeared to stay intact. He looked at Chloe for approval and she thanked him.

"Now what?" He asked.

"I will nail it in." She showed him the lid that was in place when she found it. "Thank you. I got it from here."

He nodded and just backed away. "Are you sure? Let me do that. You are too upset and I don't want you to hurt yourself," he said.

"No," Chloe said quickly, almost cutting him off. "I've got it. Thanks." She looked at him and said, "I'm sorry."

"What for?" He asked. "You have had a rough day.

Please just know that I am here for you if you need me."

"I'm just tired." Chloe looked at him with a little frustration because she knew he did not believe a word she had said. "I'm just going to take care of this and go to bed early. I guess I'll see you in the morning."

Kenneth took the hint and went out of her room and straight home. Chloe knew he didn't believe her, but at this point, she didn't care. She went and got her father's hammer and a box of nails and went to work on the securing of the box. She used about thirty nails even though it was only nailed down by four nails when she originally opened it. It took her almost an hour, but she managed to get all of the nails tightly into place. She was sweating and exhausted by the time she was done and she was surprised no one came upstairs to see what all the banging was. She stood up, covered up the box with that white sheet and walked out of her closet. She closed the door and went to the bathroom to clean herself up.

Exhausted, she went to bed.

The next few days in school were hell as usual for Chloe. No one spoke to her unless they had something negative to say like "Nice clothes!" or "Where do you get your hair done?" However, this week they added a new one to their line of questions: "Trip anyone lately?" Chloe just ignored these statements like she always did but this week they did bother her more than usual because of what happened with Piper and the fact that people were blaming her for it, even students who were not there. Chloe tried her best to ignore everyone, but one girl made it almost impossible, Jill Atwater who was Piper's best friend and the ring leader of the Barbie Doll girls now that Piper was not there. She was the one telling everyone that Chloe pushed Piper down the steps when Chloe knew she had to know that wasn't the truth because she was there when it happened. She had to have seen that Piper was behind Chloe.

The torturous nagging from her classmates came to a climax when Chloe was in seventh period - the last one of the day - on Thursday afternoon. She had almost made it through the day when two police officers came to her classroom and took her teacher out into the hall. Her teacher came back in and asked Chloe to go into the hall with the officers. The entire class erupted in "Ooohs" and "Aaahs."

Chloe went out the door to where two officers in uniform were standing.

"Miss Mattson?" the male office asked.

"Yes," Chloe responded.

"I am Sergeant Wright and this is Officer Joyce," he said. Chloe knew from his name that he must be Kenneth's dad. She hadn't met him yet because he was always at work. "We have a few questions about Miss Piper Alexander." He said as he flipped through a small tablet of notes.

"I don't know how I can help. I don't really know what happened." Chloe was starting to get upset.

"It's just routine; we are asking everyone who was there." He assured her. "Did you see or hear anything that might help us?"

Chloe was clearly getting agitated. "I don't know how she fell. It doesn't matter anyway. It's not like you are going to believe me."

Officer Joyce cut in, "Miss Mattson, I think we might have to take this down to the station."

"Why? I didn't do anything!" Chloe got really defensive.

"For your own privacy," Officer Joyce said.

Chloe agreed and went back into the classroom to get her things. Now the class was really making noise at her possible involvement. The teacher silenced them with threats of detention as Chloe continued out the door. She went down the hallway and out the front of the school with the officers to where their cruiser was parked in the parking lot. Sgt. Wright opened the back passenger side door for her so she could get in. She looked at her surroundings once she was inside and couldn't believe that the car looked just like the ones in the movies with the radios and all the gadgets on the dashboard. There was even a gate-like thing that separated her from the officers who were in the front seat. The entire scene made her feel like a criminal.

It took about ten minutes to get to the police station and the ride was a quiet one, except for the radio up front that had a woman's robotic voice coming out of it the entire time. Chloe figured she was calling for all of the police units to check in with her. They got to the station and Officer Joyce got out of the car and came to the door where Chloe was sitting and opened it. She guided her out of the car with her hand so she would not hit her head and she closed the door behind her.

"Just this way," she said as she guided Chloe in the direction of the front door to the station and told her to follow Sgt. Wright.

They went in the front door and down a hallway to a room at the end. It was a 10x10 room with a table and three chairs in the center of the room. Sgt. Wright asked Chloe to have a seat in the single chair behind the table. The two officers took the other two. Chloe folded her arms and placed her fidgeting hands on top of the table. Her heart felt like it would come through her chest at any moment and she knew they could probably tell she was nervous. They asked her if she needed anything before they got started.

"Can I call my dad?" she asked.

"Sure. You can use this phone." Sgt. Wright pointed to a phone which hung on the wall next to the door to the room. "We will just be right out here." Then he and Officer Joyce left the room to give her some privacy.

She dialed the number to her dad's shop and a husky man's voice came across the line, "Mattson's Auto."

"May I please speak with Bill Mattson?" Chloe asked. "It's his daughter."

The man didn't say anything. He just put the phone down. Chloe heard the thump it made on the table or wherever he set it. Then Bill came on the line after about a 30-second pause. "Hello?"

"Dad?" Chloe started to cry. "It's me. I am at the police station."

Before she could say another word, he interrupted her. "What? Why?" He fired questions faster than she could respond. "Are you alright?"

"Yes." She hesitated. "Well, no."

"What's that matter? Why are you there?" He asked.

"It's Piper, Dad. They think I had something to do with her fall. I swear! I didn't! I don't even know...!" She couldn't get any more words out.

"Chloe, you listen to me," he demanded. "Don't say a word. Do not answer any questions for them until I get there. You are seventeen years old, damn it!" He was mad. "It is not legal to question you without a parent present. I am leaving right now. Remember. Don't say anything and if they have a problem with that, you tell them to call me on my cell." He hung up the phone and Chloe knew it would be at least 45 minutes before he got to the station so she sat back down at the table.

Sgt. Wright came back into the room and asked if she had reached her father. She replied, "Yes. He is on his way and doesn't want me to answer any questions until he gets here."

"OK," he said. He knew her father was right. "Would you like anything to drink while you wait?"

"No thank you."

He exited the room and told Chloe he would return when her father got there. Bill must have driven fast because he arrived at the station within 40 minutes and was immediately taken to the room where Chloe was nervously waiting. She was fidgeting her hands worse than before and she stood up when her father entered the room. She looked at him with fear in her eyes because she didn't know how he was going to react seeing her in a police interrogation room. He went right over to her and hugged her which surprised her. She started to cry and the officers came in again.

Sgt. Wright started again and explained, "We just have to get a routine statement from everyone who saw the incident at the school." Then he took a device out of his pocket and placed it in the center of the table. "Do you mind if I record this session?" he asked.

Chloe spoke up right away, "No. I have nothing to hide." She reached over and put her hand on her father's hand. She hadn't shown any kind of affection toward him for a long time.

Sgt. Wright pushed the "Record" button on the recorder. "We are here today, Thursday, September 22nd, 2016 with Chloe Mattson regarding an incident that happened on Tuesday, September 20th, 2016 involving Piper Alexander and her fall down the steps at Hollow Creek High School." He sounded so official it made Chloe even more nervous. "Miss Mattson, can you tell us what you saw on that day?"

Chloe looked at him puzzled. "Yeah, I didn't see anything. I was at the top of the stairs getting ready to go down to my next class when Piper came flying next to me from behind and fell down the steps. I didn't see her coming." She spoke real fast. "I don't know how it happened! She must have tripped!" Chloe got upset and started crying again.

"Is it true that you and Piper got into an altercation not long before the event?" Sgt. Wright asked. "We spoke to a Jill Atwater who confirmed this and seems to think you may have pushed Piper down the steps."

"Yes, But. No, I didn't push her. Yes, we fought." Her answers were short and she didn't know what else to say.

"OK. That's enough," Bill cut in. "Are you arresting my daughter or what? Is she being charged with anything?"

"No," Officer Joyce spoke. "Let's all just calm down."

Bill was angry. "Then you can't hold her here and I

think we said all we are going to say." He took Chloe's hand and walked her out of the police station without looking back. They got right into his car and drove home, neither one of them said a word the entire way.

When they got home, Chloe got out of the car as soon as it stopped and went into the house and straight up to her room. She sat on her bed and opened her laptop, not that it was going to work. It hadn't worked for days. She slammed it shut and turned on some music. She was listening to the The Pretty Reckless. She played her music loud in an attempt to forget about the day's events.

As Chloe listened to the angry voice of Taylor Momsen sing, "Going to Hell" (which pretty much described how her day was going), she started to smell the aroma of something baking.

Sarah loved to bake and did it so much that the cabinets were always so full of her food and they usually had to throw a bunch of it away once a week. After about an hour, Chloe had retired to her bed to read. Then there was a light tapping on her door and she opened it. It was Sarah standing there with a plate full of her white chocolate and macadamia nut cookies, which Chloe had to admit that she absolutely loved.

"I heard you had a rough day," Sarah said.

"Yeah." Chloe's answer was cold as she took the plate of cookies and closed the door before Sarah could say anything else.

Chloe went back to her bed to lie down and read

some more. She was reading Anne Rice's *Interview with the Vampire.* She ate a few cookies and put the plate on her nightstand. Then she closed her book and drifted off to sleep early, leaving the day's demons behind her.

Friday morning, Chloe woke up with the usual beam of sunlight shining through her window and lying across her face. She rarely needed her alarm clock due to the timing of the sun. She sat up in her bed and looked at the half-eaten plate of cookies on her nightstand, feeling somewhat guilty that she was kind of rude to Sarah the previous night. All she was trying to do was make Chloe feel better after being interrogated by the police.

After getting ready for school she went downstairs to find Sarah brewing her morning coffee. Bill had already left for work due to his long commute. Chloe reached past Sarah to get a bagel and dropped it into the toaster. "I'm sorry," she said quietly as she sat down at the table waiting for her breakfast to pop out of the top of the toaster.

"It's okay," Sarah said. "I don't have to take up all the space in here, right?"

"No. That's not what I meant." Chloe sounded sincere, which was something Sarah was not used to. "I'm sorry about last night."

"What about last night?" Sarah asked, even though she knew what Chloe was talking about.

"Nothing." Chloe turned to look at the toaster as her bagel came out the top. "Thank you for the cookies." That was all she could muster up, but it was something and it made her feel a little better.

Chloe grabbed her bagel and without putting cream cheese on it like she normally did, she went outside with Raven to let her do her morning business. After letting her dog back in the house, she stayed outside and waited for Ken to come out of his house to take her to school. She didn't have to wait long before he came out of his door. She walked over to his driveway and they both got into his Honda.

"Good morning," Kenneth said. "I know you have been having a tough time lately and I want you to know that I will not pressure you to talk about anything." That was more than he had said to her at one time for a while.

"Thanks," Chloe said to him as she looked at him questioningly. "Did your dad say anything about yesterday?" She could not believe she actually got the nerve up to ask him.

"No. He does not talk about anything that happens at the station, especially when it has to do with someone we know," Kenneth reassured her. "So, are *you* going to tell me?"

Chloe looked at him as if she was going to open up to him. After a few seconds, she simply said, "I don't want to talk about it."

Kenneth completely understood and said, "OK." And they continued their journey to school, which Chloe was not looking forward to.

The day at school was pretty quiet for Chloe as she ignored most of the students as usual. That was until seventh period. That was the class Jill Atwater was in so the harassing began the second Chloe walked in.

"Trip anyone lately, bitch?" Jill asked.

"Shut up, Jill." Chloe responded as she sat in her seat and put her textbook on her desk.

The rest of the class was full of comments and cell phones dinging, which Chloe knew were students messaging each other cruel and untrue statements at her expense. She just sat and tried to pay attention to the teacher's lecture on protons and neutrons, which was something Chloe didn't give a shit about. The fifty-minute class seemed to take two hours before the bell finally rang to dismiss the students for the day. Chloe felt like everyone was watching her as she walked out of the room. Maybe it was just paranoia or maybe not. Either way, the day was over and she was out of there. She went straight out the door without going to her locker, even though there was a book in there that she needed for homework. She didn't care much about homework with everything else she had going on.

She was walking across the parking lot when she heard the loud screeching of skidding tires directly behind her. She quickly turned around to see Jill's fire engine red Mustang inches from her.

"What the hell is wrong with you, bitch?" she screamed at Jill.

"Oh, I'm sorry," Jill said sarcastically. "Were you

walking there, freak?"

Chloe slammed her fists down on the hood of Jill's car leaving a small dent when Kenneth pulled up beside her. All of the students in the parking lot were laughing at Chloe.

"Get in," he said.

She looked at him with narrowed eyes and a face that was three shades of red from anger. She was breathing heavily as her eyes flooded with tears. Kenneth got out of the car and went around it to open the passenger door for her. He almost had to force her to get in. He closed her door with her securely inside and looked back at Jill with hatred in his eyes. He then got into his driver's seat and peeled out of the parking lot.

"I was handling it!" Chloe yelled at him as they made their way away from the school.

"Really? What were you going to do?" he asked.

"I DON'T KNOW!" she screamed at him and then buried her face in her hands and started sobbing.

Nothing else was said on the ride home, and when Ken pulled into her driveway, she didn't even wait for the car to come to a complete stop before opening the door and jumping out.

"Chloe, what the hell are you doing?" Kenneth asked, but she just kept going right into her house.

Neither of her parents were home yet so she stopped in the kitchen to get a can of soda out of the refrigerator. She sat at the kitchen table, upset and sweating; she could not stop thinking about what a bitch Jill had been that day. She hated that school and hated most of the students, but she never treated anyone the way they treat her. She finished her soda, grabbed another one for later and went upstairs to do the one piece of homework she bothered to bring home.

Up in her room, she sat at the desk where the typewriter had been. She could spread her books out there now because it was not there anymore. After an hour or so, her father called her down for dinner to which she responded that she wasn't hungry and then she cranked her music up. She fell asleep to Metallica's *Enter Sandman,* which seemed appropriate.

The next day Chloe did not want to leave the house. Except for taking Raven out a few times, she had not even gone outside. By the time evening came around, she was going a little stir crazy so she went out on the back steps of her house and sat down to get some air. She gazed at the nighttime sky. It was such a clear night with a crescent moon and hundreds of stars twinkling in the night. Chloe could even make out the different shapes in the sky, made up by individual constellations. She looked at them until they all seemed to run together like an activity in a connect-the-dots workbook. She sat there for a while with her mind finally able to relax. She did not know exactly how long she was out there before she finally went back into the house. Bill and Sarah were out to dinner that night so the house was nice and quiet. She decided she was just going to get ready for bed and she went upstairs.

The bathroom was dim because one of the three lights had burned out right when Chloe hit the switch to turn them on. She stood looking at her dark eyes, dark hair, and dark lips and said to herself, *Maybe I am a freak.* She opened the medicine cabinet to get some aspirin for a low-grade headache she was developing and something fell off the shelf. It was black, but she didn't see what is was; it happened so fast. She only heard it hit the counter next to the sink and fall on the floor where she heard it skid from one side of the room to the other. She got down on her hands and knees to search for it. After crawling around for a minute, she saw something behind the toilet and reached for it but could barely grab it. With her fingertips, she was able to grasp the black piece of metal, at least she thought it was metal. She pulled it out from behind the toilet to get a closer look at it and was immediately struck with fear. Chills ran through her body when she realized it was a typewriter key. Not only was it a key from a typewriter, but it was the "J" key from the *Royal* typewriter. She squeezed it in her hand so tight that her hand started to bleed. She went into her room without having a chance to take the aspirin and she stopped dead in her tracks in front of her desk and screamed. The typewriter was back in place at her desk, there was paper loaded in it, and there was one single word typed in capital letters:

J I L L

She didn't bother going into the closet to see if the wooden box was broken that she nailed shut; she just ran straight over to Kenneth's house without looking back. That was getting to be a habit. When she got there she pounded on his back door as hard as she could with her fist until he opened it. He asked her to come in.

"No!" She screamed. "Come with me! Please, Ken,

come with me!" She pulled his arm and he didn't budge.

"What's the matter?" he asked. "You look like you've seen a ghost."

Actually, Chloe was always pale because of the makeup she wore on her face to offset the black makeup, but this was different. She let go of him and sat down on the top step to his house.

"You have to come so I know I'm not crazy," she said.

He came out the door and sat next to her. He saw her hand balled up in a fist and bleeding so he pried it open. "What is this?" She was still holding the typewriter key. "Is this what I think it is?"

She just looked up at him and nodded. "Yes."

"But that's not possible," he said. "We put it away and you *did* nail it shut, didn't you?"

"Yes." She was crying heavily now and could not get any more words out.

Ken took her hand and they walked over to Chloe's house together. Her parents still were not home, which was a good thing because they didn't want to have to explain this to anyone else just yet. They went inside and right up to her room, only this time when they got there, the typewriter was still there and the paper was still there. Although Chloe was scared, she was glad it was there because Ken had to believe her now. He just had to.

Ken looked at the typewriter for what seemed like five minutes or so; it was probably just a few seconds.

"Holy shit, Chlo! You were right!"

"See?" She was still crying. "I don't know what to do! Why is this happening?" she asked.

"And you haven't typed on this?" he asked even though he knew the answer.

"No! I did NOT do this! You have to believe me!" she yelled. "Why is this happening?"

"I don't-" He couldn't get another word out before she interrupted him.

"Listen to me!" she demanded. "This...this...thing, it's like it knows stuff!"

"What are you talking about?" Kenneth asked, but he already knew what she was going to say.

"The day Piper fell, well actually, the day *before* she fell, *her* name was typed on this damned thing!" She sounded desperate. She just knew he was not going to believe her.

"What do you mean?" He looked at her and got real serious. "Chloe, tell me exactly what happened."

"OK." Chloe took a deep breath. "The day before Piper fell we had a fight. That was the same night you and I went out to dinner. Remember?"

"Yeah," he motioned with his hand for her to continue.

"When I got home that night, I was in my room and Raven was growling at something. That is not like her at all." She started pacing the floor as she spoke. "I sat down at my desk chair to pet her and calm her down. That was when I noticed she was staring at the typewriter so I looked up to see what was upsetting her. There was nothing there." Chloe looked up at Kenneth to see if she could figure out if he believed her or not. "That was when it happened."

"What happened?" he asked.

She hesitated. "Please don't think I'm nuts," she pleaded. "Right in front of me, the keys started moving and I swear, I was not doing it!"

"Chloe," he started to speak but she silenced him by putting her finger to his lips.

"No. Please let me get this out," she said. "The keys typed out Piper's name! Then she had her accident the next day!" She was almost yelling now.

"Ok, slow down." He put his hands on her shoulders and guided her to sit down on her bed. "I have been debating whether or not to tell you this or not," he said.

"Tell me what?"

"I can't believe this typewriter is still here after all this time." He looked at the floor as he spoke.

"What do you mean?" She asked him. "Do you know something I don't? Because if you do, I'm gonna be pissed! Ken, what is the deal?"

"There was a lot of speculation after Old Lady Parrish died," he said. "Some people blamed it on her loneliness, some people said she must have had some hidden illness, but the majority of the town thought it had something to do with the typewriter she used for her stories." He looked to Chloe for a response. "I don't know what I believe."

"How could you not tell me this?" she asked. "You knew I was using this when I first moved in and you didn't say anything? Why? You even knew that I nailed it shut in that box after *you* put it in there because I was afraid of it and you *still* said nothing?" she yelled. "Well now it got out all by itself and did this!" She showed him the key in her hand again and pointed to Jill's name on the paper. "What am I supposed to do?" she cried.

He looked from the Royal to her. "You are talking about this thing as if it is human."

"Well, is it?"

"No, Chlo," he said and then he mumbled, "I don't know what it is."

Chloe put the "J" key on the desk and looked at Ken. She was really mad at him now. "Well, you have to help me get rid of it."

"I don't think that will matter," he said. "Legend has it that Mrs. Parrish made several attempts to get rid of it herself, but it was somehow attached to her and kept coming back."

"You're freaking me out, Ken! Stop!" she cried.

Kenneth took hold of her hand. "Let's go get this cleaned up before this becomes a problem as well." He went into the bathroom with her and cleaned the blood off her hand from gripping the key so hard. "Mrs. Parrish," he started, "was a lonely old woman who no one ever spoke to. She lived here alone because her husband

135

died a long time ago and left her a lot of money. I guess it was life insurance. I don't know the details, but what I do know is that she did have a part-time job at a real-estate office for a while, but beyond that, all she did was work in her yard all the time and write stories that we would see in the local magazines. My dad used to say that she was obsessed with her stories. Anyway, things started happening around here. The stories would come true from time to time and she was in trouble with the cops a couple of times because they thought she had something to do with some local disturbances."

"What do you mean disturbances?" Chloe asked.

"There were a couple of robberies that had gone bad where people got shot and there was a house that burned down a few blocks from here. I'll take you to it if you want. Everyone got out of the fire except for one firefighter. The kicker is that he was someone she was rumored to have had an affair with and her husband hated him," Kenneth said.

"Did she write about that?" Chloe asked.

"No, I don't think so but because it was Jim, the one she had the affair with who died, the police tried everything they could to make it seem like Mr. and Mrs. Parrish had something to do with the fire."

Chloe looked confused. "How do you know all this stuff?"

"When you're the kid of the sergeant, you hear a lot of stuff," he said. "The only thing I really remember seeing a story about was the robbery of the Royal Farms store on Main Street. I remember my dad reading the story to us with her name as the author and then it happened. I think it was the day after the story came out in the magazine. Everything that was in her story, right down to the store clerk getting shot and killed, actually happened. Of course, it was not a Royal Farms store in her story. I forget what the store was called, but the details of the robbery were eerily the same..." He stopped for a brief moment. "You can probably find these stories somewhere, but for now what do you want to do with this typewriter?"

"I'd like to dump it in a river or something, but you said it won't matter," she said.

"It might. I'm not sure; I don't know if Mrs. Parrish ever tried to get rid of it or not. Like I said, there were rumors," he said. "OK, there is one lake nearby. The rumors about her and this typewriter could just be a bunch of bullshit." He said that to try to make her feel better, but with everything she just told him, he wasn't so sure.

He went to get his car and the two of them carried the Royal down the two flights of stairs and out to the Honda. They put it in the backseat and covered it up with the sheet, which also seems to be a part of it. Kenneth drove to the lake and, just like he said, it was pretty close. They got out of the car once they got there and looked around to make sure there wasn't anyone there who might see them. The area was clear of spectators so they got the typewriter out of the backseat and, again, they both had to carry it due to its weight.

They got to the edge of the water and Ken explained that it was too shallow there so they should walk it out further. Chloe agreed, so they walked in about 20 feet until the water was waist high and they just dropped it. Both of them had to jump back to make sure it didn't land on their feet. Then they just stood there for a moment while cold water gushed into their shoes and clothes and they watched as a bunch of tiny bubbles rose to the surface of the water and exploded. It was as if they dropped something that was alive in there and it was letting the last of the air out of its lungs as it slowly drowned. An eerie feeling overtook Chloe as she slowly turned to head back out of the lake. "Let's go!" she said as she grabbed Ken's arm and directed him toward the embankment.

Monday morning came too fast as usual. After the dumping of the Royal, Chloe's weekend was pretty uneventful as she didn't even leave the house, not even to go over to Ken's. She felt weird about their relationship now since the events of Saturday. Even though Ken told her what he knew about the typewriter and its previous owner, she still felt like he thought she was batshit crazy. She felt like their relationship was falling apart before it even had a chance to happen.

Ken picked her up for school as usual, but she felt it was out of obligation now more than anything. They didn't talk on the ride, which was normal for them. When they got there, Chloe got out of the car and glanced back at Ken. "See ya later," she said with no emotion.

That Monday at school was another fairly quiet one for Chloe as she had not seen Jill all day, which she was thankful for because she had just about had it with Jill and the rest of the people at school who accused her of having something to do with Piper's accident. Her somewhat of a harmless day came to an abrupt halt when she got to seventh period. Everything always happened during seventh period because that was when she had to share the classroom with the Barbie dolls. Chloe thought about skipping this particular day, but didn't want detention.

When class settled in she noticed that Jill's seat was empty. That explained why Chloe did not see her all day. She wasn't even at school. She stared at Jill's desk thinking how relieved she was that she wasn't there until an uneasy feeling flooded through her body because she thought about the Royal and how Jill's name was plastered to the sheet of paper on Saturday. Chloe's attention was redirected to her teacher, who was trying to get class started by collecting homework and telling the students to get their textbooks out and open them to Chapter 5. Just then, there was an interruption over the intercom system and the class looked up at the speaker on the wall. That was when the announcement came.

"Good afternoon, my fellow administrators, faculty, and students." It was Principal Netzkey's voice coming out of the speaker. "It saddens me to have to inform you all of the sudden passing of one of our own. A tragic accident claimed the life of fellow senior student Jill Atwater late Saturday night." His voice was cracking as if he were fighting back tears. "We will be closing school for the rest of the day and there will be councilors on campus all day tomorrow for anyone who may need to talk. We are greatly sorry for this loss and will help anyone in any way we can to get through this grieving process. Thank you all and God bless."

Everyone just sat in class for a few moments staring around in complete silence. Then, a few girls cried out in pain over the loss and everyone else just started gathering their belongings slowly while they spoke of their disbelief of what happened to Jill. Chloe felt like she had been punched in the stomach. She got her things and ran out of the classroom, down the hallway, and right out the door. She kept running past the parking lot, not even stopping at Ken's car because she didn't want to see anyone, especially him. She ran as far as she could in the direction of her house until she was too exhausted to go any further so she stopped at a tree to rest.

Chloe dropped down to her knees and began to cry violently as the reality of the news she had just received sunk in. She walked the rest of the way home without stopping or looking back. Her mind was like a tornado of thoughts and unanswered questions spinning out of control. Could she have done something? Could she have warned Jill about the prediction that her typewriter made? Jill never would have believed her if she had tried and that would have only lead to more humiliation on Chloe's part. Still, she couldn't help but wonder if there was some sort of link between Jill's death and the typewriter that now sat at the bottom of a lake she didn't even know the name of and didn't care to ever go back to.

When Chloe got home, no one was there. She let Raven outside to go to the bathroom and then she walked through the living room to get to the stairs with the intention of going up to her room. She noticed her father's newspaper on the coffee table; it was the one for the current day where Jill's accident was on the front page.

The cover story headline read, "Tragic Teen Death Shocks a Community in Hollow Creek." She looked further and read the article and it mentioned Jill Atwater's name and that she was a senior at Hollow Creek High School. According to a witness, Jill's car just ran off the side of the road and stuck a tree at high speed. There were no other cars around. The witness stated that he tried to go over and help her but when he got close the car went up in flames. The witness was a man named Charles Parker and he said the worst part was the screaming. He stated, "I could hear her blood curdling screams from inside the car and I just knew she was burning. I saw her hands beating on the window, but I could not get to her. I called 911 and she just screamed and there was nothing I could do!"

The fire was so bad that her body was unrecognizable by the time they got her out of it. Chloe later learned that the authorities did not even let her parents see her to identify her because of the trauma it would have caused them.

The article mentioned that she was identified by her license (which they found intact), her car, and dental records. Chloe could not read any further; she threw the paper down on the table and went upstairs crying. She went straight into her bathroom to clean her face up and to get some aspirin because the day's events had given her a pounding heading.

What was she going to do? She kept asking herself that question as she took her aspirin and went into her bedroom where it was freezing cold as usual. She looked out her window just in time to see Kenneth pulling up his driveway. She didn't know how to approach him about this, but she knew they had to talk. He was the only one she could talk to right now about this whole crazy mess. She watched him go into his house and she decided it was now or never. She had to go over and talk to him.

Chloe grabbed a jacket and ran out of her room with Raven on her heals. She ran down the stairs and grabbed the paper to show to Kenneth before she turned to head toward the back door of her house. She ran through the kitchen, not paying attention to her surroundings as she kept her head down to make sure she didn't run into Raven. When she reached the door she was out of breath when she grabbed the knob to turn it. She looked up quickly so she could open the door and she screamed as something startled her. Standing there just on the other side of the door, she saw Kenneth whose face was almost pressed up against the window. Chloe caught her breath and opened the door to see him standing there with the same newspaper in his hand. She stepped outside and took his hand as they slowly walked down the steps that lead to Chloe's backyard.

The late September air was chilly as the time approached the early evening hours as Chloe, Kenneth, and Raven set off on a walk toward the woods where they first met. They didn't talk on the way back there, but Chloe was squeezing Kenneth's hand in a way that clearly stated how much she needed him at that moment. She was holding her jacket with her other hand and Kenneth saw that as an opportunity to start up the conversation.

"Are you cold?" He looked at her and she nodded. He took her jacket out of her hand and put it around her shoulders so she could put it on and they continued their walk in silence.

When they reached the wood line, Chloe stopped abruptly and, without beating around the bush, said, "What do you think of this?" She held her copy of the newspaper up and shook it in front of him as if she were angry.

"I'm not sure Clo, but I think it's kind of a weird coincidence. Don't you?" As he said this, Chloe wasn't sure if he was asking her or telling her. Either way, she did not believe in coincidences.

"I don't know what to think anymore," she said, "All I do know is that I wasn't a hundred percent surprised to hear that something happened to Jill; were you?"

"Honestly, no." Kenneth could not even look at her face as he spoke these words. "We did get rid of it though."

Chloe quickly said, "Yeah, but that damned thing knew something was gonna happen." Her voice was getting louder and Kenneth put a finger to his lips to shush her. "It *made* it happen!" She said.

"Do you hear yourself?" Kenneth said as if he didn't believe the same exact thing. "It's just not possible, Chloe. There's no way."

She interrupted him. "Then how do you explain Piper and now Jill?" She waited a few seconds for an answer, but when one did not come she continued. "That fucking typewriter is possessed or something!"

"Chloe, keep your voice down." He grabbed her hand and directed her further into the woods so they would not be seen or heard. "I know it's weird and creepy and way too coincidental, but possessed? That's crazy!"

"You told me about the strange things that happened with the old lady. Are you telling me now that you don't believe the typewriter had anything to do with it?" She was getting defensive.

"I don't know Chloe, but even if what you are saying is true, what can we do about it? We got rid of it and as far as I'm concerned, no one ever has to know that but us."

"That's true, but it doesn't make me feel any better." Chloe was looking down and petting Raven on the head. "I feel like what happened to Jill was my fault because I kind of knew about it."

"What would you have done?" he asked her sarcastically. "Hey Jill, I think something bad is going to happen to you because my typewriter said so." He said this imitating Chloe's voice. "Do you know how crazy that sounds? Not to mention the fact that, if you were

145

to say something, you would surely be blamed for this accident too. Is that what you want?" He sounded like he was getting mad.

"No, I guess not. I want to go home. I'm tired." Chloe ended the conversation before it was really finished but she didn't want to talk about it anymore. "C'mon Raven!" She called for her dog who had wandered a few trees away from them and they walked home.

Kenneth walked Chloe to her back door. "So, I'll pick you up in the morning?"

"Yeah, I guess." She said before stepping into her house with Raven and closing the door in Kenneth's face.

The next few days at school were intensely somber. The senior students had already constructed a collage on the main hallway wall full of memories that involved Piper before her accident and now they added photos of Jill to it. It was becoming a memorial; even though Piper wasn't dead, it just felt that way because she was not at school. The memorial made Chloe uncomfortable every time she walked past it or even just looked at it because she was starting to feel some sort of responsibility for these tragedies. She was careful not to outwardly show these feelings, however, because people already blamed her for Piper's accident. No one had warmed up to her and she wondered if it may have been different if nothing ever happened to Jill or Piper. It didn't take long for people to start blaming her for Jill's accident as well, even though she was obviously nowhere around when that happened. Stories circulated of Chloe cutting the break lines to Jill's car or messing with something inside the engine to make her car not work. Chloe wondered if the students realized how stupid they sounded when they said these things out loud.

When Chloe got home that Friday after what seemed like the longest week ever, she sat in the living room with Sarah and watched some television. Sarah enjoyed that because Chloe never wanted to even be in the same room with her. It didn't last long though, because Chloe got up without warning and just went to her room. She sat in there doing homework and listening to music when she noticed something strange. A dim light was emanating from under her closet door. She kept her closet closed all the time now because of the whole typewriter thing. She looked at the light which was getting brighter by the second as she looked at it. She thought maybe she left the closet light on, but this light was too bright for that. It was as if someone was shining a flashlight or something through the crack between the closet door and the floor as the beam of light lead across the floor and shined directly on Chloe's foot, which was dangling over the side of her bed. She slowly got up and walked to the door and when she opened it she saw where the light was coming from. It was the box, the one the typewriter was in. The mysterious light came out of the top of the wooden box and Chloe realized she didn't put the lid on it when they got rid of the typewriter. Raven came up behind her and started barking violently at the luminous box. Chloe was shaking but she had to check it out. She walked over to it but as soon as she got there it disappeared and the inside of the box was pitch black. She looked at Raven, who ran out of the closet as if she was chasing something. Chloe reached over and grabbed the lid to the crate and threw it on top of it before running out of the closet too.

"You saw it right?" The dog's ears went up and she cocked her head to one side like she always did when

Chloe spoke to her. She took Raven downstairs to take her for a walk. "How about some air, girl?" She patted her on the head and Raven got excited and wagged her tail as they went out the back door. Chloe needed some air as well to wrap her mind around what just happened.

She decided to go for a walk around the neighborhood with Raven instead of through the woods like last time. She was more familiar with the area now. They walked down their street and cut off onto a couple of side streets that Chloe hadn't been on yet. She wanted to check them out. The old style Victorian houses faded into smaller, one-story ranchers the farther they got. There were people mowing lawns, checking their mail, and some were just getting home from work and pulling up their driveways. The yards were smaller, and for a moment, Chloe wished this was where they moved to instead of Honeysuckle Drive. She lived around people who had money and were kind of stuck-up, except for Kenneth. His family had money, but it didn't make him act any different. While she walked and thought about these things, Raven started pulling on her leash and barking.

"Hey girl, what is it?" Chloe asked her, but she just kept on barking. "Raven!" Raven stopped barking but continued to tug Chloe across the street as her barks turned into growls.

Chloe finally looked over and noticed there was another dog on the other side of the street with its owner.

He looked like a black lab, but Chloe couldn't be sure. The dog's owner was also pulling him back because he had started yanking her across the road to where Chloe and Raven were. The dog's owner was a girl who looked to be about Chloe's age, but that mixed with the fact she also had a big dog wasn't what really got Chloe's attention. This girl looked like she shopped at Hot Topic (Chloe's favorite store) and her long black hair had green streaks down the back. She also had her nose pieced and the upper right corner of her lip pierced. Chloe had been asking her father if she could get her nose pierced and of course he always said no. The girl and her dog walked toward Chloe.

"Hi. I'm Nikki Patterson," she said as she tried to maintain control of her dog. "And this beast is Buddy." She giggled as she introduced the dog.

"I'm Chloe and this is Raven." Chloe responded. "I'm sorry if she bothered you." She usually didn't speak to people this easily but something about Nikki made her feel comfortable.

"Oh no! It's okay." Nikki was nice. "I love her. She's beautiful. I always wanted a German Sheppard." Nikki reached over to pet Raven. "Is she friendly?"

"Oh yes. She loves everyone," Chloe said as she bent down to scratch Raven's head. "Don't cha, girl?" She played with her a bit.

Nikki was also petting her dog. "Do you live around here?"

"We just moved in around the corner."

"Oh really?" Nikki asked. "Which house?"

"It is a red Victorian house around the corner on Honeysuckle Drive." Chloe didn't have to say another word. Nikki knew exactly which one she was talking about.

"It's not the old Parrish house, is it?" she asked.

"Yes, but I'm starting to wish it wasn't."

Nikki's look changed somehow. "Why? It's a nice place."

"Because everyone seems to know of it and from what I understand, the old woman Parrish, was a little weird and may have died in the house." Chloe tried to explain.

"Oh, don't let your neighbors tell you crap." Nikki was almost angry. "Yeah, Mrs. Parrish wasn't liked by too many people, but that's only because they didn't get her."

"What do you mean?"

"They didn't understand her," Nikki said. "I liked her because, like me, she was different."

Chloe was deciding in her head as Nikki spoke that she really liked this girl and was glad she ran into her. "Hey. Do you live here?" She pointed to the rancher that Nikki and Buddy were standing in front of before they came over to introduce themselves.

"No." Nikki said. "It's the one over there." She pointed to a brick rancher with a big yard and an attached two-car garage. "That's where Bud and I live."

"I haven't seen you in school." Chloe asked this sort

of question-like.

"I do classes at home," Nikki explained. "Screw that school. No one liked me and I didn't like them so my parents took me out. I am home schooled now."

Chloe mumbled under her breath. "I wish I could do that. I hate those people." Then she got louder. "Everything is so messed up now!"

"Yeah, I know what you mean." Nikki said, "I probably would have put a gun to my head if I had to stay there."

The girls both laughed and started walking together to the side of the road Nikki's house was on when a woman came out of her house and called her in for dinner.

"That's my mom." Nikki said and she started pulling Buddy away to head home. She turned her head back toward Chloe. "Hey, do you want to come in and eat? My mom won't care."

Chloe looked surprised. No one ever invited her to dinner at their house, at least not in a real long time. "Sure. My stepmom probably won't even notice I'm gone."

The girls went to Nikki's house and walked in the front door with her mom. "This is Chloe," she said to her mom. "I invited her to dinner." That was all she had to say and they took the dogs to the fenced in backyard and went in and sat at the kitchen table. "Don't worry. Buddy is fixed."

Chloe answered, "So is Raven."

The Pattersons' home was nothing like the Victorian houses on Honeysuckle Drive, but it was nice. In fact, Chloe liked it more. The front door lead directly into the living room where they had a large flat screen television, a leather sofa, and a reclining chair to match it. There was a hallway to the left where the bedrooms were and probably the bathroom. They walked straight through the living room to an opening that stepped into the eat-in kitchen. It looked like they had a dining room next to it also, but there was a desk in there and some bookshelves so it looked like they used it for an office. There was an aroma that filled the house of amazing scents that told Chloe whatever they were having for dinner was going to be great. Mrs. Patterson wore one of those white kitchen aprons with little ruffles around the bottom and a tie that fastened in the back. The kitchen table was already set for two people when the girls got in there and Mrs. Patterson kindly placed another place setting in front of Chloe. "You like meatloaf?" she asked.

"Yes," Chloe said. "I haven't had that in a while."

"Well good." Mrs. Patterson smiled. "Then you are in for a treat because I made meatloaf, mashed potatoes with gravy, and green beans. It's Nikki's favorite," she said this as she glanced over at Nikki. "Where do you live, sweetie?" She was so nice.

"Over on Honeysuckle," Chloe said.

"Oh. Did you move into the Parrish house?" she asked.

"Yeah. Everyone seems to have known that woman," Chloe said as her eyes drifted toward the floor.

"Yes. Nikki used to hang around with her sometimes and help her do her yard work. We appreciated the friendship she showed our daughter," Mrs. Patterson explained as Chloe looked at the empty seat at the table where there was no place setting. "Nikki's father is working later tonight. He is a lawyer and gets stuck at the office quite a bit."

Chloe didn't know what to say. "Thanks for letting me eat over here, Mrs. Patterson."

"Honey, it's no problem. I don't see many of Nikki's friends."

Nikki cut in at this point. "That's because I don't have any, Mother!" She wasn't very nice when she said this.

Mrs. Patterson put the plates of food on the table and told the girls to help themselves because she was going to wait for her husband before she had dinner. Chloe and Nikki both started piling food onto their plates. Chloe felt right at home there. They could hear the dogs playing in the yard and they seemed to be getting along great so they ate dinner until they were stuffed to the gills and put their dishes in the sink. Mrs. Patterson said she would take care of them.

"Want to go to my room?" Nikki asked Chloe.

"Sure," Chloe said as they walked to the door all the way at the end of the hallway.

Nikki's room was dark. She had lights on her ceiling that she dimmed with a switch on the wall and black curtains hung in the windows to keep the sun out. She had a double bed and a computer table just like Chloe's and a small dresser, which she had covered up with stickers that named rock bands. Chloe was the most impressed with the huge poster of The Pretty Reckless that was on the wall opposite to her bed. She immediately went over to it.

"You like them?" Chloe asked with a big smile on her face.

"Yes. I got that poster at a show earlier this year," Nikki said. "I saw them twice during their *Going to Hell* tour this year, once in New Jersey and once in Virginia."

Chloe got excited. "I was at the Jersey show. Aren't they great?"

Nikki went over to her dresser where she had speakers hooked up to an iPod that was already programmed to play music from The Pretty Reckless. She started the music and the girls sang the song *Follow Me Down* along with the band and they laughed and smiled at each other because they knew they had just become friends. They had so much in common. Chloe just wished that Nikki was in school with her so she would have someone to talk to there. After listening to the music and talking for about an hour, Chloe said she had better get home with Raven before it got dark. She also knew in the back of her mind that her dad didn't even know where she was and she was sure he was home by now.

The girls exchanged cell numbers and Chloe walked home where Bill was waiting for her.

"Where were you?" he asked. "We were getting worried. You and Raven should not be wandering around the neighborhood. You don't know it that well yet."

"What do you want me to do, stay in my room all the time?" Chloe asked sarcastically. "I can't hang out down here with your wife."

"Chloe, you know that's not true," he said. "I wish you would give Sarah a chance. We've been married a year now. Don't you think it's time?"

"Time for what? To forget about Mom and the way we used to be a family?" Chloe was mad.

"Stop it, Chloe! You know I don't want you to forget about your mother. Neither do I. This grudge you have against Sarah has to stop. What happened to Mom was not Sarah's fault. We didn't even know each other then."

"Didn't you?" Chloe knew Sarah used to bring her car to his shop to get it worked on. "I think you did. Stop lying about it, Bill!" She knew he had an affair while her mom was alive and she thought it was with Sarah. She also knew that her mom knew and that's why she was upset that night.

"What do you mean, Chlo?" he asked.

Chloe screamed, "MOM KNEW!"

She ran upstairs before he could respond.

Chloe was crying in her room when she heard a soft tapping on her door. She dabbed her eyes with the sleeve of her shirt in an attempt to hide this, although the black streaks of eye liner that were getting to be a constant thing lately were evident on her right cheek. Surprised to see Kenneth walk in, she asked, "What are you doing here?"

"Nice to see you too," he said. "Your dad let me in. He said you guys had a fight and that I should come right up because you probably wouldn't answer him if he called you downstairs."

"Well, at least he was right about one thing," she snapped. "He's such a jerk sometimes. So why are you here? Is something wrong?" She looked away from him.

"No. I just wanted to see you. Why does anything have to be wrong?" he asked. "Chlo, if you want me to leave, I will. I can see you have been crying and I hope you know that I am here for you." He sounded sincere, but Chloe didn't believe him, not entirely anyway.

"It's just that you don't come over much anymore. I am always the one to come over to *your* house. I feel like you are mad at me like everyone else at that stupid school." Her eyes narrowed as she spat these words at him.

He quickly reached over and grabbed her hand as

she tried to pull away from him. "Actually, I came over because of that reason."

"So you *are* mad at me!"

"No, Chloe. I came over to tell you that I am not. I haven't seen much of you this week other than the rides to and from school so I thought you were mad at *me.*" He gently squeezed her hand.

She pulled away. "Here's a secret, Ken! I *am* pissed at you actually! We had sex and things changed right after that. The only time we talk is when I come to you and tell you about the messed up things that are going on around here!"

"That's not it at all, Chloe. I am not like that!" Now he raised his voice. "You know what? Think what you want..." He headed toward the door to leave.

"Stop!" she said. "Wait." Her voice got softer as she went over to him and closed her door locking the two of them in her bedroom. "I didn't mean it. I was just pissed at my dad." She reached up, pulled his head to hers and kissed him softly on the lips.

"I'm sorry." She kissed him again.

Ken pulled away. "What are you doing?"

"I've missed you. We are friends, right?" she asked as she took his hand again and led him to her bed.

"Are you sure about this, Chloe?" He was confused. "Your dad is right downstairs and just a minute ago, you accused me of using me."

"I don't care!" she snapped at him and pushed him down on the bed.

Her forcefulness turned him on as she climbed on top of him and started to unzip his fly. He put his hand there as if he were going to stop her, but he knew he wanted it just as bad as she seemed to. The only problem was that this didn't seem like Chloe at all. Kenneth looked up at her and the expression on her face was one of anger and it almost scared him. She pushed his hand aside and reached over to her dresser where her iPod was and turned it on. Metallica was what came on her Pandora station and she turned it up just loud enough so that it would muffle any sound the two of them might make. She took control and slid her hand down his pants straight into his boxers and grabbed him with such force that he jumped up, pushed her off, and got off the bed.

"What the hell are you doing? That hurt!" he said.

Without answering him, she looked him in the eye and smiled, licking her lips. Then she stood up and took her clothes off down to her black lace panties and moved toward him as if she were floating. He stepped back but she thrust toward him, grabbed him, and started to sloppily kiss him all over his mouth. Her strength was unnatural and, although he tried, Kenneth could not escape her grasp. The more he resisted, the stronger she got. She turned him back toward the bed and launched him back onto it with one quick push.

"Chloe, STOP!" he shouted.

Chloe put her index finger to her lips and she got back on top of him. "Shhh...'

Kenneth was scared and he started shaking. "Get off me! I don't know why you're acting this way." He was looking right into her eyes and felt like she wasn't even hearing him. "GET OFF!" he shouted as he pushed her upward with both of his arms.

That triggered something in her because her body went somewhat limp and he was able to get out from under her. He stood up next to the bed as she just sat there staring at the floor. Kenneth gathered his clothes and quickly started to put them on when Chloe started crying. She looked up at him with confusion in her eyes. "What happened?" she asked.

"You don't remember?" He was aggravated and she could hear it in his voice.

Chloe was still crying. "I have a terrible headache and why are my clothes on the floor?" Suddenly, her look turned to one of fury. "What did you do?"

Realizing the whole scenario was about to be turned around, Kenneth tried to defend himself. "Nothing! This wasn't me, Chloe! It was you; don't you remember?"

Chloe's facial expression started to change. She was still crying, but she appeared to be searching through the air for her thoughts. She looked at Kenneth and back down to the floor and softly said, "I think I blacked out." She picked her head up to see his reaction to this. "I remember you coming into my room and then, nothing."

"I don't know what's going on here, Chloe, but if

you are messing with me-"

She interrupted him, "No! I'm not! What happened here?"

He picked up her clothes and handed them to her. "Get dressed. I just came over to see how you were doing and you started acting really weird. You attacked me, Chloe." He was calm now because he believed she was being truthful. He just knew there was something going on here and they had to get out of this room. He sat next to her on the bed as she finished pulling her socks on and put his arm around her.

Chloe held him tighter than she has ever held anyone. "I'm glad you came over," she said. "I'm sorry for..." She wasn't sure exactly what she was apologizing for since she could not remember what had just happened. "I'm sorry for everything. Can we go for a ride or something?"

"Sure, where do you wanna go?" he asked.

"I don't know. Can we just drive?" she said. "I have something to tell you and I don't want to talk here."

He nodded yes and they went over to his house and got into his car and drove without any particular place in mind. He turned on some low music and drove out of the neighborhood. He kept glancing over at her as if he had something to say, but was afraid to. After they drove for about fifteen minutes with Chloe sticking her head halfway out the window to get some air, he spoke up, "Have you had any more trouble with... ya know?"

"Maybe I am going crazy." She put her head down

and looked at the floor of the car.

Kenneth put his hand on her leg and patted her knee. "I don't think you're crazy. Maybe a little fruity..." They laughed and she put her head back.

"Ken?" She got serious. "What do you know about Mrs. Parrish?" She wasn't ready to tell him about the light yet.

"What do you mean?" he asked. "I didn't know much about her, only that she worked at some office that sold real estate. She wasn't an agent; I think she was just a secretary or something, but didn't I tell you this already?"

"Yeah, but do you know where it was?" Chloe asked him. "And did she do anything else? I mean, did she go anywhere?"

He looked at her confused. "I think she used to volunteer at the county library also. Why all the questions? She didn't really do anything when I knew her because she was always writing. Everyone used to say she was so obsessed with writing that she never came out of her house unless she was working. I know at the end there, she wasn't even working. I feel like I've told you all of this already," he said.

"Did she get too old to work or something?" Chloe asked.

"I don't think so. Actually, I remember hearing about some falling out at her job and she quit without warning." He tried to remember the details. "But you know how people talk. A lot of people didn't like her so

I don't know what is true and what isn't."

Chloe looked disappointed because she wanted to know more than he had to offer. "Do you know anyone who might be able to help me?"

"What is it that you need help with?" he asked. "Is something wrong?"

"I'm not sure. I think she might have something to do with the weird things that have been happening with that typewriter." Chloe started to get anxious. "Think about it: didn't she used to use it all the time, and when it was found in her room, wasn't there something typed on it? I don't know, some word or something? It's almost as if she was typing when she died."

"What? Are you talking ghosts?" He pulled the car into a parking lot of a convenience store. "

"I don't know what I'm talking about. I just need to talk to someone."

"There might be a lady. I used to see her take walks with Mrs. Patterson," he said. "She lives around the corner from us."

"Do you mean Nikki's mom?"

"Yeah. How do you know her?" he asked.

"I don't really. I did just meet Nikki earlier today when I was walking Raven. She had her dog out too," Chloe said. "We got talking and then she invited me to dinner. That's when I met her mom. I only saw her for a short time though, but she spoke a little about Mrs. Parrish. So, you know Nikki?"

"Yes. I mean I used to. She doesn't come out much

anymore, not since she dropped out of school," he said.

Chloe looked at him. "She is being homeschooled because the stupid people at that school didn't like her, just like they don't like me." She defended Nikki. "She's nice and I think I might hang out with her more."

"If you do, then you should have no trouble talking to her mom," he said. "From what I heard she has no problem when it comes to flapping her gums." He laughed a little. "She used to gossip about a lot of things. I think, at one time, she worked with Mrs. Parrish."

"Perfect. Thanks," Chloe said. "That little bit of info just might be what I was looking for."

They drove home after talking for a little while; it was getting late. Chloe didn't want to go home to see her father, but she was tired. When they got to her house, she leaned over and kissed Ken before she got out and ran up to her door. She went inside and right to bed where she couldn't sleep due to the new information she just received. She couldn't wait until morning so she could go over Nikki's again and, this time, possibly talk to her mom.

The next morning was Saturday so there was no dreadful school to go to, which was good because Chloe didn't get much sleep due to nightmares she started to have that involved Jill. She dreamt of her burning inside her car and she was screaming Chloe's name. In her dreams, she could see the flames licking the car windows and the roof of the car from inside it while they surrounded Jill's burning face. Chloe saw what was left of Jill's charred face right before she woke up from the horrible dream.

Chloe got out of bed that Saturday morning with those images still clearly displayed in her head. She opened her bedroom door to the aroma of coffee and bacon which helped take her mind off the dreams. Well, there had to be something with it, but the aroma of bacon was so wonderfully overpowering that it usually cut everything else out. She figured it was probably eggs. Either way, someone was making breakfast and she was starving. She hesitated at the top of the steps, debating in her mind what to say to Bill. She hadn't spoken to him since their fight the previous day, but she had to get over that if she wanted to partake in the meal that was occurring downstairs. She slowly descended the stairs and went into the kitchen. Bill and Sarah were both cooking. Sarah was scrambling a large skillet of eggs and Bill was flipping the crackling bacon. Chloe went over to the coffee pot and poured herself a cup of coffee without saying a word to anyone, so Sarah turned her head from the pot she was working with and smiled at Chloe. "Good morning," she said.

"Good morning." Chloe still sounded groggy from sleep.

Bill finished up with the bacon and carefully placed it on a plate which was covered with a paper towel to soak up the grease. Then he placed the plate on the table and got some plates and silverware out of the cabinet and put them on the table as well. Chloe took them and spread them out so the table was set. Bill got himself a cup of coffee and sat at the table across from Chloe and she noticed that he looked like he didn't know what to say to her either.

Chloe made it easy for him because she just wanted to eat and go to her new friend's house. "Dad, I'm sorry about yesterday. I've just been so stressed lately with school and everything that's going on."

"I know," he said as he plated up some food for himself and for her. "It's OK. Can we just forget it?"

"Yes. Please."

They finished breakfast and it was actually nice; they spoke of the move and the new house and what they did and did not like about it. Chloe told them the house was growing on her, but she hated the school. She knew they didn't think much about that statement because she hated the last school she attended also. Bill used to tell her to stop dressing and looking like a zombie if she didn't want to be harassed. He stopped when he realized that was just her way of expressing herself and the more he said anything to her about it, the more she would change her hair or wear more makeup because she thought it pissed him off. He just gave up after a while and accepted it.

People at school were different though; they always had to have that one person who they tormented because they thought it was funny. It was usually the girls who were the worst. The guys just went along with it to be a part of their clique. Chloe figured they would get theirs one day because she believed strongly in karma. It was this belief that made her want to look into Mrs. Parrish and the typewriter further because she was a little freaked out that two girls who bullied her seemed to have been affected by it, although she would like to think it was just a coincidence. With these thoughts in the back of her mind, Chloe excused herself from the table. She had somewhere to be and didn't plan on telling them about it. She just knew she wanted to go back to Nikki's house and try to find out some information as far as anything Mrs. Patterson could tell her about Mrs. Parrish.

27

Chloe knocked on the Pattersons' front door and Buddy started barking right away. No one came so she knocked again because there was a car in the driveway. Buddy sounded like he would come right through the door with his vicious sounding bark, but Chloe knew better. He was a very friendly dog. Mrs. Patterson finally came to the door and opened it when she realized it was Chloe. She had to get Buddy under control. She said he didn't usually act like that. She grabbed his collar and directed him into another room, and after a few minutes of coaxing the Labrador, she opened the screen door and let Chloe in.

"Hello," she said. "Chloe, is it? My memory is so bad when it comes to names. I apologize."

"It's no problem. Yes, it's Chloe. You remembered." Chloe smiled.

"I'm sorry, but Nikki is not here. She is out with her father."

Chloe looked down at the floor as if she was embarrassed. "Actually, I'm here to see you, Mrs. Patterson."

"Really, what about?" She looked concerned. "And please call me Carol. Mrs. Patterson just sounds so formal." She smiled.

"OK, Carol, I wanted to ask you something," Chloe said as she fidgeted with her hands. "I was wondering if you knew Mrs. Parrish before she died." She quickly asked the question because she knew she would chicken out if she hesitated.

"You mean the woman who lived in the house you moved into?" she asked.

"Yeah. That's the one." Chloe slowly raised her head and made eye contact with Mrs. Patterson.

"I worked with her a long time ago and we remained friends almost up until the day she disappeared." Mrs. Patterson just started talking like she had been waiting to talk to someone about her old friend. "We worked in a small real estate company where I actually used to sell houses and she answered phones. There were only about five of us who worked there at any given time. I actually was the one who sold her that house on Honeysuckle Drive. She was living by herself in a rundown apartment and her husband had left her a bunch of money when he died so I talked her into getting a nicer place."

Chloe interrupted. "Why did you suggest such a big house when she lived by herself?"

"She liked the Victorian style homes and she was a writer and loved to read. She had a ton of books so she made two of the bedrooms into mini libraries. Actually, she loved books so much that she volunteered at the county library."

"Yeah, I heard that from someone." Chloe said.

"Anyway, since I helped her move into this neighborhood and she was so close to me, we got to take long walks every day after work. She was amazing. She created a huge garden in her backyard which she singlehandedly kept up. I don't know how she managed it with her work and volunteer schedules while writing her stories."

"What did she write about?" Chloe asked.

"Most of her stories no one saw because she was so private. She did publish a couple thriller/mystery types, but only two, I think." She looked like she was getting a little sad. "Why are you asking me all of this?"

"You will probably think I'm weird, but I think I feel her around the house," Chloe said. "Or, I feel something. I'm just not sure what it is." Chloe was surprised she had just told Carol this. She barely knew her.

"Tell me something," Mrs. Patterson said. "Where is her typewriter?"

"Why?" Chloe asked.

"She used to tell me some things about that thing. She was so obsessed with it right up until the end."

"It was in my room but I got rid of it."

"Why did you do that, Chloe?"

"Things happen when it is around," Chloe said.

"What kind of things?" Mrs. Patterson's facial expression changed from one of happiness to one of looking frightened.

"Bad things."

The look in Chloe's dark eyes scared Mrs. Patterson to the point she felt the need to take a step back. "Does this have something to do with what happened to those girls at the high school?"

"I don't know!" Chloe got real defensive. "I don't know!"

"I'm sorry, hun. Calm down," Carol said.

"Where is there a real estate office around here?" Chloe asked. "I don't remember seeing one."

"Oh, it's not around here. It's about a half hour or forty-five minute drive from here in the town of Clairemont," she said. "A little place called Humphrey's Homes."

Chloe immediately felt a lump in her throat as her heart dropped from her chest to the pit of her stomach. She knew that place all too well. First of all, she used to live in Clairemont with her mom (when she was alive) and her dad. Second, her mom worked at Humphrey's Homes also. Either Carol was talking about the same place or there were *two* little places called Humphrey's and they both sold homes in the small little freaking town of Clairemont, which didn't seem likely. Chloe was betting on the first scenario.

That wasn't all: when Carissa worked there she often complained of one of her coworkers who, Chloe just knew, *had* to be the slut that was sleeping with her father. Although, Bill didn't know his wife knew about the affair until Chloe blurted it out last night. Carissa told Chloe of the woman right before she died in one of her drunken stupors. She drank a lot when Bill started cheating on her. She didn't know what she was saying half the time and normally wouldn't tell her 14-year-old daughter that her father was screwing around on her, but she did just that one night and Chloe even still remembered the slut's name. It was Carol. Chloe felt sick as she suddenly realized she was standing in front of the woman who tore her family apart.

"I have to go," she said, and she left quickly without looking back. She had so many thoughts running through her head on that walk home. What should she do? Should she talk to Nikki anymore? The biggest question on her mind was whether or not her father knew that this woman lived around the corner and if he knew Mrs. Parrish. Is that why he bought this house? Does Sarah know? Chloe was confused and didn't know what to do, but when she got home she had an overwhelming feeling that she wanted to go fish that typewriter out of the water because it might know some of these answers. But how would she get it? Once again, she was going to have to ask Ken for help. Just as quickly as that thought came into her head, it went right back out. She could get it herself.

When she got home, Chloe got dressed in jeans and her combat boots which she thought would be the best way to get into the water. She remembered that the lake was pretty close and she thought she remembered how to get there so she just walked. Once she got there, she walked over to the embankment and looked around. She couldn't remember exactly where they dropped it in. She stood there for about three or four minutes looking to her left and right until she saw some bubbles form on the surface of the water. She knew that was the place she dropped it. Was this thing actually helping her find it?

She started to walk into the water, and as she got closer to the area where the bubbles were, they increased. By the time she reached them, that part of the lake looked like a rapidly boiling pot of water. She reached down as far as she could but didn't feel anything where she was standing. She had to go under the water because it was down too far for her to reach. She looked around to make sure there were no people there and she dropped herself down under the water and found the typewriter. Regardless of its weight, she carried it out of the water and put it on a rock. For some reason, it did not feel as heavy as it was before.

She thought about how she would manage to get the typewriter home so she sat next to it for a while to rest before trying to walk home with it. Breathing heavily from the exertion of her carrying it out of the water, she put her head down and rested it on her arms, which were folded over her bent knees. After only a few minutes, she picked her head up and looked to her left only to be stunned. The Royal was gone! All that remained was the watery outline of where she placed it on the rock. Chloe looked everywhere for it and came to the conclusion that someone must have stolen it while she wasn't looking. She didn't know how that was possible because she was right there and she didn't hear or see a thing, but that was the only thing that made a little bit of sense. She was upset but realized there was nothing she could do so she walked home.

Chloe stopped at Ken's house before going into her own. She was still soaked from her excursion in the lake.

"What happened to you?" he asked.

She looked down at herself and then lied, "Oh. Nothing. I was walking and someone's sprinklers came on."Kenneth laughed at this and invited her in to dry off. He got her a towel and one of his t-shirts. She changed in his bathroom and looked in the mirror to see that her hair was all flattened also. She tried to brush it with his brush that was sitting on the counter, but it was too knotty. She put the brush down and noticed something black on the floor in the corner next to the toilet. She bent down to see what it was and she couldn't believe it. There was an ink ribbon spool, which looked like the one from her typewriter. She picked it up and it was damp. Immediately, she blamed Ken for taking the typewriter while she wasn't looking. She stormed out of the bathroom and walked right up to him. "Where is it?" she yelled.

"Where is what?"

She put her hand in front of him. She had the ribbon gripped inside of it and she opened it to expose the black ribbon, which bled onto her hand.

"What the hell is that?" Ken asked.

"It was in your bathroom! You tell me!"

"Chloe, I have no idea what that thing is. I've never

seen that before." He sounded sincere and she could tell he probably wasn't lying.

She kept the ribbon and walked to her house telling him she would return his shirt by the next day. She walked away and left Ken stunned on his back step.

Back at her house, Chloe went straight upstairs without acknowledging Bill and Sarah sitting at the kitchen table. She didn't want to answer any questions about why her hair and makeup were a mess and why her jeans were wet. She placed the ribbon on her desk and got in the shower to wash the remnants of the lake out of her hair. When she got out, she wrapped herself in a towel and went back to her room, still partially dripping. She froze in the doorway. Not only was her room freezing again but her typewriter was comfortably sitting on her desk. She almost dropped her towel, but instead, she went over and sat in her desk chair so she could get a good look at it. The "J" key was back in place and she could see where the ribbon was missing. She picked the ribbon up to study it to see if it was suitable to be put back in or if she needed the new one. She figured she would try so she put it back down on the desk and got up and went in her closet to get dressed. She was a little concerned as to how the Royal made its way back home, but she wasn't going to dwell on it. She wasn't going to question what that thing was capable of anymore.

All dressed, Chloe went back to her seat to put the ribbon back in and the ribbon was gone. She looked on the floor and everywhere, but didn't see it. Then she looked in the Royal and couldn't believe it. The ribbon was back in place and didn't look damaged or anything! She did some play typing to make sure it worked and then she started typing for real. She didn't even know why.

Chloe typed and typed and before she knew it she had written a five-page story. She didn't even know what it was about. The Royal took over her hands and she just let them go. She needed to get out of that place for a while and, mentally, she did. She didn't know how, but she did.

She released the last page out of the Royal and put it on top of the other four she didn't remember typing. She looked at her watch to see that it was 3:00 p.m. and she realized she had been typing for well over an hour. She decided to read the story and she was amazed with what she saw on the pages. She had constructed a story about a dog attack on a woman. It was so violent it scared her that she would even have those thoughts in her head. It was a pretty good story though so she put it aside into a folder. She knew how to get the rage out of her body now when she was upset. She got up from her chair and went downstairs where she could hear her dad moving around. He was in the living room surfing TV channels so she thought now was as good a time as any.

"Bill?" she asked.

"Yes, hun," he answered. "What's up?"

"I don't know how to bring this up, but I have to know. Does the name Carol Patterson sound familiar to you?" she asked him as she noticed his facial expression completely change.

"Why are you asking me this, Chloe?" he asked. He wasn't even looking at her when he spoke.

"Did you know she lives right around the corner from us?"

"No, I didn't and can you please just drop this before Sarah gets home?" He was obviously nervous.

"Why?" Chloe got mad. In her mind, he had just confirmed that he knew her. "You planning on cheating on her too?"

"Don't you talk to me like that!" He was furious. He walked out of the room which only made Chloe more upset. "How do you know her anyway?" he asked while he walked into the kitchen.

"Because I made friends with her daughter, *Dad!*" She was crying. "I didn't know who they were and now, how am I supposed to face Nikki again when I hate her mother?" Chloe screamed. "I finally make one friend I can truly relate with, and I am going to lose her before I ever have the chance to get to know her!"

"Chloe, it was three years ago!" he hollered.

"I DON'T CARE! It still hurts just as if it were yesterday," she yelled at him. "Your affair killed mom and you know it!" She took Raven and ran out of the back of the house.

She ran to the tree line behind their house and sat

there with her dog. She cried until she had no more tears left and it got dark. Then she went inside and went to bed. It was early, but she didn't want to see anyone else that day. Chloe went to bed that night hating the entire world, except for Raven.

Monday at school Chloe was more quiet than usual. The memorial wall grew with more photos, balloons, and decorations to highlight Piper and Jill's moments at the high school. The students were starting to get on with their studies and not be so sad all the time; that was, except for the rest of the Barbie Doll clan. There was Brenda, Jennifer, and Victoria who all left Chloe alone at this point because they were afraid something might happen to them. That's what Chloe thought anyway. Although Chloe knew that she didn't personally do anything to the other two girls, she liked having that kind of power over the rest of them because it kept them away from her. She didn't care if they still blamed her; at least they were finally leaving her alone. The rest of the students seemed to be also.

Chloe walked home from school that day to get some fresh air. It was a chilly afternoon, but the cool breeze mixed with the warmth of the sun felt good on her face. She still had the events of the weekend weighing heavily on her. Her route to her house seemed different now because she had to go past the Patterson house and she didn't want to see that woman again. The closer she got to their house the angrier she felt inside. As she approached their street she stopped because she saw a black Ford Explorer in their driveway. She watched as her father came out of the front door with Carol who was crying. Chloe thought he must have told her what she figured out. Now she knew she couldn't go back there because it seemed that her suspicions had just been confirmed. Carol *was* the woman he cheated on her mom with and she was pretty, which did not help matters. Chloe then became sorrowful for Carol's husband. She wondered if he knew about it. She had not met him yet because he was not there whenever she went over to the house.

Back at her house, she let Raven out and got a soda before going up to her room. She did not want to see Bill at all. Up in her room it was so cold she was forced to turn the heat on for the first time that season. It wasn't even autumn yet. She had her own thermostat in her room so she could adjust it to any temperature she wanted. She turned on some music and started her homework, and after about an hour, she put her books aside and drifted off to sleep.

Carol Patterson was doing dishes in her kitchen later that Monday evening when she heard a noise like breaking glass outside. She knew her husband and Nikki were not home and their dog Buddy was inside with her so it couldn't have been one of them. It sounded like one of her plants fell off the front steps or something. She thought it was probably the pot that broke because she thought she definitely heard something break. She opened her front door and immediately discovered she was right. There was broken glass and potting soil all over the front walkway. Unhappy about the mess and the loss of one of her good flower pots, she went to get a broom and dust pan to clean it up. When she went back out the front door, she closed it behind her so Buddy would not get out.

Carol squatted down to sweep everything into the dustpan with her back facing her yard so she never saw it coming. Before she knew it, she was face down on the brick steps with an animal snarling and scratching at her back. It was all she could do to get turned around to face her attacker in order to try to fight. She screamed and waved her arms in every direction, but the more she fought, the more aggressive the animal became. Her blood curdling screams and flailing arms did not even phase the creature.

Frightened for her life, Carol shielded her face and body with her arms while she was repeatedly bitten and maimed by a dog (at least she thought it was a dog) she could barely see because her eyes were closed for most of the gruesome assault. Her mind was intact enough that she wondered why none of her neighbors heard her screams and she also knew her cell phone was inside so she couldn't even try to call 911.

The force from the dog was so fierce that she couldn't even begin to get it off her. The arms she used as shields were turned into cuts and hanging flesh which dripped blood all over her and the surrounding sidewalk. She could no longer hold them in front of her so she opened up her face for one long scratch that went from her forehead to her chin, catching her right eye. She instantly saw blood run into her eye, and she became weak and woozy.

After battling with the beast for a few minutes, she could not fight anymore. She curled up into a fetal position on the concrete walkway that lead to her house while the dog continued to bite her arms and face for a few seconds before it finally ran away.

Carol was barely breathing and there was a blood trail from the broken flower pot halfway down the Patterson's walkway when Nikki and her father got home and found her. Her face was unrecognizable and Nikki screamed and called 911 on her cell phone right away. They sat with her until the paramedics got there and they each held one of her hands as they hoped and prayed she wouldn't die. Nikki was hysterically crying as her mother was near death in her arms.

When the ambulance got there, the crew jumped out with all kinds of equipment and loaded Mrs. Patterson onto a stretcher. She stopped breathing so they initiated CPR and Nikki was so scared at the way they pushed on her chest and put the mask over her bloody face. It looked like they were hurting her more as they desperately tried to save her life.

By this time, some of the neighbors came out to see what was going on and Mr. Patterson started yelling at them. "Didn't anyone hear her? What's wrong with you people? Did anyone see *ANYTHING?*"

He got in the back of the ambulance after they loaded her in and he rode to the hospital with her. He told Nikki he would call her as soon as he could. All she could do was go inside and wait; she was so scared, but she did as he asked and went inside where she found a little comfort with Buddy as they sat and waited for news.

Chloe woke up Tuesday morning shivering from the cold. She only had a light sheet pulled over her and, apparently, turning the thermostat temperature up did not warm her room up at all. After sitting up in bed and rubbing her eyes, she looked down on the floor next to her bed to nudge Raven awake so she could let her outside. The dog was not there. She got out of bed and went over to her window to see if Raven was already outside. She didn't see her, so she started to doubt herself. She could not remember whether or not Raven was with her when she fell asleep because she had fallen asleep so early the previous night and she was more worried about trying to stay warm than anything else.

After only a minute or two, Chloe remembered she never let her dog back in after she let her out to pee the previous night. Her mind was so preoccupied with anger toward her father that she actually forgot about her dog. She had never done that before and felt horrible about it. She ran downstairs and went out back but Raven was nowhere to be found. Chloe walked up and down Honeysuckle Drive frantically looking for her. She called her name a few times before she started to cry because she couldn't find her best friend. With feelings of defeat she walked back home and sat on the back step of her house. She put her hands over her face and started to cry as thoughts kept running through her head. What was she going to do without Raven? How could she be so stupid? Then Chloe thought that maybe Raven wandered off into the woods behind their house so she stood up and looked back at the tree line. That was when she saw her. Raven was lying down back by the woods. Chloe ran back to her smiling and calling her name, but she just laid there licking her legs.

When Chloe got to Raven, she noticed that she was cleaning herself with such intent because she was covered with mud or something. It wasn't until Chloe reached down to pet her that she noticed the coppery scent which she could not explain until she got real close to her dog and noticed she was covered in something that looked like it could be blood. "What's the matter, girl?" Chloe asked her as she searched her body for cuts or anything that could explain all of the blood. She realized Raven did not have any wounds so she took her home and cleaned her real good with a hose and her dog shampoo. She managed to get her completely cleaned off and just figured Raven must have gotten into a fight with an animal in the woods or something since that's where she found her. She felt sorry for the other animal because it looked like Raven got the better end of the deal.

Chloe felt so bad about leaving Raven out all night that she spoiled her the entire day. She took her for a long walk, she played ball with her, and she had access to an unlimited supply of dog treats that day until they were both so tired they went into the living room to watch some television. Chloe sat on the sofa with Raven resting comfortably at her feet. It was 5:00 p.m.

When Chloe turned on the TV, the local news was just starting and the top story came on immediately with the words "Special Report" flashing on the television screen. The same blonde woman who seemed to report on all of the major events in the city -Chloe wondered if they had any other news reporters at all - stood in a residential area reporting on something Chloe could not quite make out. She noticed the house the woman was standing in front of and pointing at looked a lot like Nikki's. Actually, it was Nikki's so she turned the volume up to hear the report.

"It appears that Mrs. Patterson may have been outside sweeping up a broken plant when the attack occurred. As you can see the broom and remnants of the mess are still scattered by the steps at the front door." The camera zoomed in on those objects as she spoke. "Anyone with information as to the whereabouts of the animal, it is believed to be a dog, is urged to call the Hollow Creek Police Department at 410-555-3179, or simply dial 911. Do not approach the animal as we believe it is dangerous."

She continued, "Once again, Mrs. Carol Patterson is in critical, but stable condition at this time at Hollow Creek Memorial Hospital. She has been severely disfigured in a vicious dog attack and the animal is still on the loose. There were no witnesses to the attack so we do not know the breed, but we believe there will surely be some remnants of the attack on the dog." The camera zoomed in on the bloody path up the Patterson's walkway.

Chloe turned off the report at that point. She couldn't watch any more of it; she just stared at the black screen not quite sure what to think or do. She looked down at Raven who was sleeping and wondered if she could have done that. It would certainly explain the blood all over her, but Raven wouldn't hurt a fly. It just didn't make sense so she vowed to herself never to tell anyone the condition she found her dog in that day. She wasn't going to let anyone take her best friend away from her.

The next couple of days at school were somber once again, but this time it was because everyone was afraid of what happened in their neighborhood. There was talk of the cops doing a house by house search of any household that included a dog. This scared Chloe, but she knew she had done a good job cleaning up Raven of anything that might look suspicious. Just to be sure, she went back outside after hearing the news report to make sure she had cleaned the ground of anything red that might resemble blood. She also made sure the hose didn't have any residue on it and then she gave Raven one final good check from her nose to her tail. She was glad she did because about an hour after she got home from school on Wednesday, there was a knock on her door. She was upstairs with Raven when her father answered the door and called her downstairs.

She came down without Raven. "What's up?" she asked.

Sgt. Wright was standing in the doorway with Bill.

"Where's Raven?" Bill asked.

"She's up in my room. Why?"

"Has she been out by herself at all in the last couple of days?" Sgt. Wright asked.

"No. Of course not!" Chloe got defensive. "I don't let my dog out without supervision!"

"Are you sure?" he asked.

Chloe got smart with him: "I think I would know if my dog got out, Officer."

"We have to take a look at her," he said.

Chloe looked at Bill as if he should say something to save her from having to turn her dog over to this man. Bill finally spoke, "Go get her, Chloe." She got mad and stomped upstairs. She reappeared at the top of the steps with Raven a few minutes later and they walked down together, Chloe tightly holding her collar. When they got to the bottom of the steps, Sgt. Wright went over to Raven and started petting her. She licked his hand in return, which was her normal friendly manner. He checked her fur over, lifted up her tail, and her face to expose her teeth. She tolerated the entire exam beautifully. He patted her head when he was finished. "Good girl," he said. "Do you know of any other dogs this size close by that may have been involved in the attack down the street?" he asked Chloe.

"No, sir," she answered with relief. She knew that he did not think Raven had anything to do with it and they were in the clear.

Sgt. Wright left after that. He seemed satisfied as he drove off in his cruiser. Chloe went back to her room and remembered that story she had typed. She picked the pages up off her desk and read them again, but this time she noticed more about the details. The story was exactly what just happened to Mrs. Patterson and chills ran through her body as she thought, only for a second, that she might have caused the entire thing. She tore up the pages in hundreds of little pieces so no one would ever find the story and think the same thing. Then she stood up and glanced at her typewriter. She took a step back as she read the words that were displayed on a freshly loaded sheet of paper:

Now no one will want her!

After that, Chloe knew for sure the typewriter had a power which she did not understand, but for some reason it linked itself to her. It was like her protector or something and she wasn't sure she wanted that, but it excited her at the same time.

Chloe decided if she wanted to find out more about the woman who ruined her parents' marriage, who was now in the hospital fighting for her life, then she would have to go to the place where she thought the answers to her questions would most likely be.

The next Saturday, after a stressful week of school with everyone on edge over the local dog attack, Chloe asked Ken to drive her to Clairemont so she could stop by the real estate office where her mom used to work so she could try to talk with a few people who might remember her. She wanted to find out more about Mrs. Parrish and her relationship with her mom, Carissa. Ken was happy to spend the day with Chloe because he felt things had been weird between them lately and some time away from the neighborhood might do them some good. He agreed to take her and to buy her lunch, although he didn't know the details of what she had found out about Nikki's mom and her dad yet. He picked her up Saturday morning and they didn't tell anyone where they were going. Chloe wanted it that way and Ken thought it was probably a good idea since he felt his dad didn't approve of Chloe anyway and he did not want *that* hassle.

The two of them made the 45-minute drive to Clairemont and Chloe pointed out a few things to Ken along the way like her old school, her old house, and a Wendy's fast food joint that she and her mom used to go to a lot before she died. She directed him to pull onto the main drag and onto a side street which took them directly to Humphrey's Homes. It was open because there were cars in the parking lot and Chloe could see someone sitting at a desk inside the front window, not to mention the sign on the front door that read: *Come on in. We're open!*

She hoped Mr. Humphrey would remember her. She was fourteen the last time he saw her and she looked completely different back then. She always had her hair nicely braided and she was always dressed nice. At that age, she was still under the parental rules as to what to wear and Carissa always made sure she looked good.

Ken and Chloe parked his Honda and got out. Chloe hesitated as she walked up the walkway with him because she saw Mr. Humphrey standing by the front door with a man. They walked up the brick steps in the front of the building and went inside. There was no hiding as a dangling bell jingled when they came through the door. They walked right past Mr. Humphrey without even looking at him in an attempt not to interrupt his conversation. It didn't work though, because he looked right at them. It looked like he was finished with his business with the man anyway because he turned and left before the front door was even fully closed.

Chloe did not hesitate for fear that she might chicken out of the whole thing. "Mr. Humphrey?"

"Yes?" he answered. "How may I help you?" He did not seem to recognize her.

"I'm Chloe Mattson." That was all she had to say and he came right over to her and gave her a hug.

"Well, I'll be..." He smiled. "Chloe Mattson. I haven't seen you since..." He placed his index finger on his chin and looked up into the air for the answer to that.

"Since my mom's accident." Chloe said.

"Yes. I'm so sorry, dear." He was so nice. He always treated her like she was his niece or something. "What brings you here? I heard you and your dad moved away?"

"Yeah, we did. I wondered if I could speak with you for a few minutes about when my mom worked here." She said.

"Of course, hun. Anything." He was more than willing to speak with them. "You kids want a soda or something?"

They both responded, "No thank you."

"You guys can wait in my office." He pointed to his office even though Chloe remembered where it was. "I'll just be a minute. I have to sign some paperwork."

Chloe and Ken waited in Mr. Humphrey's office making observations of all of the plaques and certificates on the walls. He had run a very successful real estate business. Chloe noticed a photo on a bookcase shelf of Mr. Humphrey and her mom at some picnic or something. The picture brought tears to her eyes.

Mr. Humphrey walked into the office while she was looking at the picture. "That was a company picnic we had in the summer of 2010," he said. "We used to have a couple of those a year to keep up morale around the office, ya know?" He picked up the photo for a few seconds and then replaced it on the shelf. "So how have you been, Chlo?" He used to call her that just like everyone else who was close to her.

"I've been okay. I miss my mom a lot, but I am actually here to ask you about someone else who used to work here. I'm pretty sure she worked here when my mom did. Do you remember an Isobel Parrish?"

"Mrs. Parrish?" he asked. "Did you know her?"

"No. We just moved into her old house. I thought you might know something about that. Was it one of the houses your staff was selling?" she asked.

"No. We don't do anything in that neighborhood. I know where it is, but it's out of our area," he said. "Why do you ask?"

"I met another woman in our neighborhood who also worked for you and I think she knew Mrs. Parrish. Do you know Carol Patterson?" she asked.

He got quiet and just looked at her like he didn't know what to say. "She also worked here back then," he finally said. "They all worked here at the same time."

"Do you remember if Mrs. Patterson and Mrs. Parrish were friends at all?" Chloe sat up straight in her chair as if his next answer was the most important so far.

"From what I remember, Mrs. Parrish was more of a friend to Carissa, your mom, than she was to Mrs.

Patterson," he said. "They went to lunch together all the time. Why all the questions?"

"I found an old typewriter in our new house and I think it belonged to Mrs. Parrish," Chloe said. "At least I feel like she is connected to it."

"She still had that thing?" he asked. "Man, she used to talk about it all the time. Everyone in here thought she was nuts!"

"What did she say about it?" Chloe asked.

"She used to tell stories about how she was able to type things with her typewriter and make them come true." He laughed. "She used to tease some of the guys around here. She would say things like they better leave her alone or she would give them a stomach bug or something." He continued. "The only one who somewhat believed her was your mother. Your mom and Isobel got real close before she died... and before the other accident."

"What other accident?" Chloe asked.

"Well, I don't think your mom liked Carol, that's Mrs. Patterson; actually, I know she didn't like her much. Although, I never did know why," he said.

"Mr. Humphrey, what other accident?" she asked again.

"Carol was in a pretty bad car accident that put her out of work for a while," he said. "That's when your mom and Isobel really started hanging out a lot and they were so secretive about what they were doing and where they were going. I always thought it had to do with that typewriter."

"How so?" Chloe asked.

"I overheard Isobel talking to your mom once about trying it out; typing, I mean. I got the impression your mom wanted to type on it because of all of the things her friend said about the stories coming true." He looked into the air as if he was trying to remember more. "Yeah, I remember now! Your mom borrowed the typewriter. I don't know; maybe she wanted to write a story or she had to type something else up."

Chloe stood up and grabbed Ken's hand. "Thank you, Mr. Humphrey. We have to go now, but it was great to see you." She and Ken both shook his hand and they were out the door.

"What was that about?" Ken asked. "Why did you jump up like that?"

"Don't you see?" Chloe opened the car door anxious to get out of there. When they were in the car, she continued, "My mom made Mrs. Patterson's accident happen."

"Chloe, that's crazy," Ken said.

"Is it? She borrowed the typewriter, the accident happed, and she was friends with Mrs. Parrish. It all adds up!"

"Why would she do that?" Ken asked.

"Weren't you listening?" She was frustrated with him. "She knew about the affair between Carol and my dad and she wanted her out of the picture."

"Listen to yourself!" Ken said. "Do you know how

crazy this sounds?"

"Ken!" she yelled. "I also wanted her out of the picture and she got hurt again!" Chloe was crying heavily. "Do you think that Mrs. Parrish knew my mom was going to get into that accident?"

"How could she?"

"I don't know but who was she trying to help?" Chloe asked, still crying. "Didn't you say there was one word typed on a piece of paper when they found Mrs. Parrish's typewriter? And how come it keeps typing random people's names and then something happens to them?"

"I don't know. Try to calm down," he said. "There has to be an explanation."

"Ken! They happen to be people who have harmed me!" she screamed. "How do you explain that?" She looked at him as if she had seen a ghost. "What was the word, Ken?" She cried. "Was it 'Carissa?'"

"I don't know, Chloe!" he yelled back and then they got silent.

After a long pause from their conversation, Ken put his hand on her knee and said, "Chlo, it's gonna be alright. We'll figure this thing out."

"What if that was it, Ken? What if the typewriter betrayed her and went after her friend?" She was sobbing. "MY MOM!"

"I said we will figure it out," he said as he leaned forward and turned on the radio.

Chloe sat back, crossed her arms, and pouted. She

was surprised to hear *Follow Me Down* come blasting out of the speakers. She tried hard not to let it show that she was happy to hear that song, but she could not believe he had gone out and bought a CD of her favorite band. She looked at him and simply said, "Sorry."

He smiled. "Well, since you like them so much, I thought I better get to know some of their music. I have to say, Chlo, I like The Pretty Reckless. Good choice in music."

She gave him half a smile and they made the journey home.

Back in Hollow Creek as they got closer to home, Chloe and Kenneth noticed some police cars parked at a couple of the houses where they knew large dogs lived. They figured they must still be looking for the dog that attacked Mrs. Patterson. Kenneth turned onto Honeysuckle Drive and sped up in hopes that no one would see them, especially his dad whose cruiser was parked in front of the Gardner's house. Mr. and Mrs. Gardner were a quiet couple who did not bother anyone; actually, they were hardly ever home, but they did have a husky. Kenneth thought they had just gotten it about a year ago, but the dog was always inside, except for the early mornings when Mrs. Gardner took her walks. He could not even imagine that dog being responsible for the attack. There was no way.

With those thoughts he turned to look at Chloe and softly said, "I have to ask you something."

"What?" She asked.

"Did Raven have anything to do with what happened to Mrs. Patterson?" he asked.

"How could you even ask me that?" She avoided answering the question, got out of the car, and slammed the door shut.

"Chloe! Wait!" he shouted as she was walking away from him.

She turned back and he could see the tears streaming down her cheeks as she sobbed. He got out of the car and went over to hold her. She struggled and tried to avoid his comforting which only made him grab her more firmly. Unable to fight him, she realized she had nowhere to go and no one else to talk to. The only thing she could do was the one thing she wanted to do so she opened up to him and told him the truth about how she found Raven that morning. She made him promise not to say anything. He swore he would keep her secret because he knew now that he loved both Chloe and her dog, even though he could not say those words to her yet. She kissed him and told him he better go home and give her some time to think about what to do with everything she learned that day from Mr. Humphrey. He didn't want to leave her alone, but she insisted so he went home and she went inside where she saw Bill cooking dinner and Sarah was not home yet.

"Where is Sarah?" she asked.

"She had to go to the school for some kind of meeting or something. I don't know; it was a last minute thing," he said. "Are you hungry? I'm cooking but I can't promise that it's gonna be any good." He laughed. "Where have you been anyway?"

"Went for a ride with Ken."

"You two are getting pretty close, aren't you?" he asked.

"Yeah, he's OK," she said and then she went up to her room.

Chloe went straight to her dresser to put on a sweatshirt because it was cold in her room. She turned around and went over to her desk and she suddenly got sick to her stomach. She ran to the toilet where she knelt down and threw up a yellow, mucous-like substance that she figured was just stomach acid due to the way it burned her throat. She had not had much to eat that day. Ken treated her to lunch, but she did not eat it. She was too overwhelmed with information from the day. After she had expelled the contents of her stomach into the toilet, she stood up and wiped her face with a wash cloth and rinsed her mouth out. She leaned on the sink and waited to see if she was actually finished because the feeling of nausea was still lingering in her.

Satisfied that she was done, she walked back into her bedroom with her arm wrapped around her belly. She lied down on her bed and closed her eyes. She thought she was probably just anxious due to everything that was racing around in her mind and she regretted telling Kenneth about what she thought Raven had done.

Chloe lain on her bed and sobbed for a straight hour before getting up to go get something to eat for dinner. Bill had been cooking when she got home so there had to be a plate for her. There always was, even when she said she wasn't hungry, her parents made sure there was food left for her. They knew she would eventually come and get it. This time was no different; there was a plate of beef noodle Hamburger Helper. It wasn't gourmet, but it was one of Chloe's favorites and possibly the best her dad could put together without any help from Sarah.

When she was finished eating what little bit she could force down, Chloe decided she wanted to go see Piper at the hospital, even though she probably would not be welcomed with open arms there. She didn't know why she suddenly got the urge to go, but she had probably been one of the only people who had not seen Piper since her fall. She walked back over to Kenneth's house because whenever she wanted to go somewhere, she had to ask him to take her. How else would she get anywhere? She would get a car one day, but for now he had to be her chauffeur.

"What's up, Chlo? Did you forget something?" he asked.

"No," she said. "You're gonna think I'm crazy, but I thought I should go see Piper at the hospital."

"Why?" he asked. "You barely even know her and she was so mean to you."

"I just think, with everything going on, I want to try to keep my nose clean and if I go see her; maybe your dad won't think I had something to do with her fall."

"I'll take you if you want, but I'm pretty sure he is convinced now that you were not involved," he said.

"I'm also curious. I think I want to see for my own eyes how badly she is hurt," Chloe said.

"Alright, let me grab a jacket and just let my mom know where we are going. I was getting ready to have dinner with her."

"Oh. I don't want to interrupt that. Eat first if you want and then we'll go." She felt bad for asking him now. She knew his mom spent a lot of time alone because his dad worked so much.

"No. It's OK," he said. "I will just ask her to put some aside for me. Are you hungry by chance? She can set you a plate too."

"No thank you. I just ate with my dad."

Kenneth went in to talk to his mom while Chloe waited on the back step. He was only gone for a couple of minutes and then they got in his car and drove to the hospital. It was a short drive so Chloe didn't really have time to think about what she would say to Piper or anyone else that might be there for that matter. She thought about it while Kenneth searched for a spot in the visitor's parking lot. He parked the car and could tell something was wrong by the frightened look on Chloe's face.

"What's the matter?" He asked.

She looked at him and asked, "What am I going to say to her?"

"I think it will come to you when we get up there to her room. If you want, we can stop in the gift shop and get her something. Maybe a gift will help break the ice," he said.

Chloe liked that idea so they went in the front doors of the hospital and followed the signs to the gift shop. Of course, Chloe didn't have any money so she asked

Ken if he would mind spotting her the cash to buy a cute little pink teddy bear she saw on a shelf. He did and they made their way to Piper's room. They had to ask a woman at the information desk where to go. It was room 5154 which meant it was on the fifth floor somewhere. The old woman pointed them to the elevators and said they could follow the signs from there. That is exactly what they did.

Chloe got more nervous the closer they got to the room. There was a large nurse's station with about six or seven nurses running in and out of it for medicine, blankets, pillows, and whatever else the patients on their floor might need. Kenneth saw Piper's room and pointed it out to Chloe. There were a few people standing outside her door, who Chloe could only assume were family members of Piper's because they definitely were not students at the school. They got right next to them and Chloe hesitated. Ken looked at her and decided he would have to be the one to make the introductions.

"Excuse me," he said softly to get their attention. "Is this Piper's room?"

A man who looked to be about the same age as Kenneth's dad said, "Yes, it is. There is a nurse with her now so no one can go in for a few minutes. Are you friends of Piper's?"

Kenneth reached out his hand to shake the man's hand. "Yes...Well, acquaintances, I guess. We just know her from school and wanted to see how she was doing. I'm Ken and this is Chloe." He introduced them and they all shook hands.

Chloe was very uncomfortable standing there with Piper's family. She felt like everyone was staring at her; well, they probably were. Most people gawked at her because of how she looked most of the time. She actually had a skirt on because she made it a point to dress nice to go see Mr. Humphrey earlier. She lightened up on her makeup and her hair was in a neatly pulled back pony tail; she did have her combat boots on, though. There was a woman with long blonde hair sitting in a chair next to them while they chatted outside Piper's door. She didn't say anything and she appeared to be crying a little. Chloe could not tell for sure, but she had a tissue in her hand on her lap. The woman was pretty and Chloe thought she had to be Piper's mom because she looked a lot like her.

The nurse finally came out of the room and said visitors could go in now. Piper's dad stepped aside and told Chloe and Ken to go in because they hadn't had a chance to see her yet. He said the family would give them some private time while they went down to get a cup of coffee or something. They even asked if Chloe or Ken wanted anything from the snack bar. They were such nice people. Chloe and Ken declined the offer and made their way into Piper's hospital room.

As they went slowly into Piper's room there was a methodical beeping sound coming from a couple different machines and the sound of something that sounded like shocks being tested in an auto mechanic's workshop. Chloe assumed it was a machine helping Piper breathe; although, she thought she was doing better and did not need to be on breathing machines anymore. They could see one of Piper's legs pulled straight out and lifted into the air by a crane-looking thing. It was in a cast so it was obviously broken. As they got closer to her, they could see her face, which still had bruises on it and it looked like she had two black eyes, which were healing to a light greenish-yellow color. That must have been because her nose was broken. Her eyes were closed so Chloe thought she was sleeping and quickly went over to the windowsill and left the teddy bear there. She then gave Ken a look that told him she wanted to get out of there. Just then, a sound came out of Piper like she was trying to say something. Chloe looked at her and was scared as to what she might say.

"What are you doing here?" Piper asked. "You are the last person I thought I would see."

Chloe looked down at the floor; she did not want to make eye contact with her. "I'm not sure actually," she said. "I wanted to see how you were doing, I guess."

"Why?" Piper asked. "I was so mean to you." She started to cry.

"It's OK, Piper," Chloe said. "That's over. I got you that bear over there." She pointed to the bear on the windowsill.

"Thank you," she said. "Look at all of these things in here." She pointed around to all of the flowers and balloons and gifts. "People keep sending me stuff. It's nice and all, but it won't make me walk again."

"I'm sorry, Piper. I heard." Chloe didn't know what else to say. "Piper? You know I didn't..." She stopped short of asking what she came to ask.

"Chloe. We didn't see eye to eye, or maybe it was just me being me as usual, but I know you did not do this to me." Piper was sincere. "My parents are just looking for someone to blame this on." She started crying. "I'm not even upset about it anymore. I'm more upset about Jill than anything and my parents aren't even letting me mourn the loss of her with all of their questions about my fall."

Chloe thought that maybe that was the reason Piper's mom didn't say anything to them when they got there. She was blaming her for this. She sat down in a chair next to Piper's bed and they actually had a nice conversation for about fifteen minutes until her parents came in and said it was time for visitors to leave so Piper could get some rest for the night.

It had been a long day and Chloe didn't realize it had gotten to be 8:00 p.m. She and Kenneth said their goodbyes and asked Piper if there was anything they could do or get for her. Piper did ask for one thing. She had a picture of her and Jill in her locker and she wanted to have it with her in the hospital. Chloe said she would get it so Piper gave her the combination to get into the locker and they left.

On the ride home Chloe was a lot more talkative than she had been all day. She felt like a huge weight had been lifted since they went to see Piper. She also felt good about it because she was going to bring her a photo to make her happy. Chloe wasn't really sure where these feelings came from because she despised Piper in school; actually, she despised everyone in school. She just hated it there. She told Ken she would get the photo on Monday and asked him if he could take her back in a couple days to give it to Piper. Of course he agreed and he dropped her off in her driveway, gave her a kiss, and went home.

When Chloe went inside, Sarah was home baking as usually. She walked over and stuck her finger in Sarah's mixing bowl and got a big gob of chocolate chip cookie dough on her finger and stuck it into her mouth. Sarah was surprised but didn't say anything because she didn't want to ruin Chloe's mood. She was never in this good of a mood, not around her anyway. Chloe then went into the living room where Bill was watching TV and gave him a kiss on the cheek. He looked at her with a great big smile on his face.

"What's gotten into you?" he asked.

"Just in a good mood," Chloe said. "Is there a problem with that?"

He quickly responded, "No! It's just nice to see. Where were you anyway?"

"Ken and I went to see Piper at the hospital."

"Isn't that the girl who fell at school?" he asked.

"Yeah. We just wanted to see how she was doing."

"And how is she?" he asked.

"She's okay. I mean, she's paralyzed and all, but she seems to be okay mentally," Chloe said. "She asked me to do a favor for her so I need to get into her locker on Monday."

"That's good, Chloe. I'm glad you went out there," he said. "It seems to have done you some good."

She kissed him again, said goodnight, and went upstairs. She thought that for the first time since all of this bad stuff started happening, she would get a peaceful night's sleep because she finally felt good inside. She got upstairs and kicked her shoes off. It was cold (as usual) in her bedroom so she went to get some fluffy socks out of her dresser drawer. When she turned around to go back to her bed she saw the typewriter. It was sitting on her desk and she felt like it was looking at her.

She walked over to the Royal, not by choice; her legs just moved toward it and before she knew it, she was sitting in her desk chair. One of the keys moved by itself and punctured the paper that was already fed into the feed roller leaving a cleanly typed "K" before the key released itself back into place. Chloe sat there unable to move. She tried to get up but she was stuck as if some force was holding her in the chair. She watched as the machine controlled itself while the keys continued to maneuver themselves without any assistance. The next one to fly forward and plant itself on the paper was the "E" and then it went back into place like the first one did. It was so cold in the room now that Chloe's breath exhaled a white frosty cloud over the Royal. After a few breaths of expelled steam into the air, another key made its journey to the paper and planted the letter "N" before it went back into place like the other ones did. This continued four more times until the page's contents were complete. Chloe's heart leapt from her chest to her throat as she gasped and screamed at what was displayed on the page. "NOOO!"

The page simply read:

KENNETH

Chloe woke up on the floor next to her computer desk without any memory of how she got there. She slowly got up and there was a severe throbbing sensation in her head as if she was hit over the head with a baseball bat or something. It was aching so badly she could not even pick it up all the way as she held onto it with both hands. She felt the back of her scalp and there was a bruise or something that hurt like hell. All she could figure was that she had fallen or passed out. She was still in the clothes she had on the previous night. She looked at her watch and it was 7:25 a.m. Realizing it was the next day, she gathered herself and got up to get ready for school. Ken usually picked her up by now, but he wasn't there yet. She looked out the window and had to shield her eyes from the sun due to the pain that was piercing her left temple. His car was in his driveway so she didn't miss him. She struggled to get her clothes on and went to the bathroom to find some aspirin. She grabbed the bottle, opened it, and tossed four pills into her mouth. After washing those down with some water, she quickly brushed her teeth, touched up her make up, and threw on her combat boots. She didn't even tie them before running downstairs to wait for Ken. She waited until 8:00 a.m. before she figured something must be wrong; he was so late.

Chloe decided to go over to his house to see what was taking him so long because he hadn't even called her to say he would be late. She thought he probably overslept just like she did.

Mrs. Wright opened the door when Chloe knocked and looked concerned. "Hi, Chloe. Kenneth isn't going to make it to school today," she said. "He is not feeling well."

"Oh. Is he okay?" Chloe asked. "I was with him last night and he seemed alright."

"He woke up about 2:00 a.m. throwing up. He has a high fever and he says he hurts all over," she explained. "I am taking him to the doctor in a little while. Do you need a ride to school? I can take you if you want." Mrs. Wright was so nice.

"No, that's OK. My dad can do it. Please tell Ken I was here and I hope he feels better."

"Thanks, Chloe," she said. "I will keep you posted as to how he is doing."

Chloe went back to her house and went up to her room to get her jacket because she forgot it and it was a little chilly outside. That was when she saw the letters and the memory of the previous night's episode came flooding into her mind like a tsunami crashing into an unsuspecting shoreline. Kenneth's name was on the paper. She hoped with every ounce of being inside of her that this had nothing to do with him being sick. She put the thought aside for the moment because she had to and went downstairs and had Bill drive her to school. She was going to need a note from him anyway explaining why she was late. They were not very forgiving when it came to that kind of thing. When they got to school, she asked him to pick her up at the front door at 3:00 p.m. so she could go right home and check on Ken. She was worried about him.

Chloe could not concentrate all day: one, because Ken was home sick as a dog; two, because she may have caused it; and three, because she had to get into Piper's locker to get that photo but didn't know how she would get it to Piper now with Ken being sick. She would just have to wait for him to get better now because she was not about to ask anyone else. It took her half the day but she finally got to Piper's locker and opened it and the photo of Jill was right on the inside of the door. Just then, there was a tap on her shoulder. Chloe jumped and turned around quickly to see Nikki standing behind her.

"What are you doing here?" Chloe asked. She knew Nikki did not go to that school.

"I came in so I could fill in Mr. Netzkey on how my mom is doing," Nikki answered. Then she gave Chloe a weird look raising her eyebrows and asked, "Why haven't you been around? I haven't seen you since my mom got hurt."

Chloe changed the subject. "How is your mom anyway?"

"She lost so much blood she needed a transfusion and her face is so badly mangled that they have it completely covered with bandages. I don't even know what she looks like under there." She started to cry. "She is still in critical condition and now she has some kind of infection. I don't know, Chloe. How could this happen?"

Chloe gave her a hug in an attempt to try to comfort her. Chloe could not tell her what she found out - not now or ever, for that matter. She turned back to face Piper's locker and grabbed the picture she wanted and explained to Nikki why she was doing that. Then she thought she might be able to get Nikki to take her to the hospital to give it to Piper because she was always going to the hospital to visit her mom anyway.

She turned to Nikki. "Hey, can I ask you a favor?"

"Sure. What's up?" She asked.

"Ken has been driving me everywhere since I don't have a car and I have to get this picture to the hospital to give it to Piper," she said. "I just thought if you might be going there anyway, I could hitch a ride with you."

"I thought you couldn't stand Piper," Nikki said.

"I couldn't, but I feel bad now," she said. "I saw her and she really can't walk. I don't know how I would handle something like that."

"Yeah, I guess," Nikki said. She had enough on her mind with what her mom was going through. "I'm going there after dinner tonight if you wanna go. It'll be around six or so."

"OK. That sounds good," Chloe said. "That'll give me time to eat also. I will walk over to your house. Is that okay?"

Nikki was quick to respond, "No! My dad doesn't want anyone over. He is not doing well with this. I will come and get you."

"I understand. I guess I'll see you tonight then."

Chloe closed Piper's locker and they went their separate ways. Chloe didn't know how she was going to handle going to the hospital with the girl whose mom was attacked by *her* dog.

Chloe had a quick dinner with Bill and Sarah and nervously waited for Nikki to pick her up that evening because it was almost 6:00 p.m. She stood peering out the front window and looked for Nikki's car. She wasn't really sure what she drove, but there had been a small black car in the driveway when she visited her house. Chloe assumed that was Nikki's. She didn't have to wait long before a tiny, three-door black Kia pulled up the driveway. Chloe went out to meet her so she wouldn't have to get out of the car. They pulled out of the driveway and Nikki looked like she had been crying.

"Are you alright?" Chloe asked.

"My dad just called. He is at the hospital." she said. "Mom's not doing so well. There is an infection that got into her blood. Dad said I should get there as soon as I can."

Chloe knew that wasn't good. She must be in bad shape if the family is being asked to hurry up and get there. She looked down at the floor not knowing what to say. She had an overwhelming feeling of guilt. She hated the woman for what she did to her family, but she didn't wish this on her. Chloe just hoped and prayed the entire way to the hospital that she would be okay. When they got there, Chloe went with Nikki to her mom's room before going to see Piper. Nikki looked like she needed someone to be with her and Chloe felt so bad. They rushed through the halls until they reached the room where Carol was staying and Nikki's father was standing outside the room with his face down into the palms of his hands. He was obviously crying.

"Dad?" Nikki let him know she was there. "What is it?"

Nikki's dad just looked at her. "I'm sorry, sweetie." And they hugged.

Chloe felt so guilty and out of place. Nikki's mom had obviously just died and she knew why. She stood there for a while not saying anything; she knew exactly what it felt like to lose a mom unexpectedly. Then Nikki broke from her father's grasp and demanded to go see her mom. Her dad and a nurse agreed to let her in, but she did not want to go by herself.

"Chloe. Will you go in with me?" she asked.

Not able to say no, Chloe said, "Yeah, sure." And took her hand as they went in together.

Carol Patterson's entire head was bandaged up and she had wrapping on both arms. Chloe couldn't tell if they were casts or just bandages. She was covered up by blankets from the waist down. There were breathing tubes inserted into her face, but none of them were making any noise. Even the heart monitor was off. There was nothing but silence in the room until Nikki burst out into tears. Chloe tried to comfort her but didn't know how other than to give her a hug.

"May I have a minute alone with my mom?" Nikki

asked Chloe.

"Sure. I will go to Piper's room and give her this photo," she said. "I'm really sorry, Nikki." She rushed out of the room.

Chloe went down the hall and to the elevators to go up to the fifth floor. Mrs. Patterson was on the fourth. She quickly went up and there was no one at Piper's room this time, probably because it was getting too late. Piper thanked Chloe for the photo and said she was sorry for picking on her in school. Chloe said not to worry about it and she hoped Piper was able to get out of the hospital soon. They said their goodbyes and Chloe went back downstairs.

Nikki was still in with her mom and Chloe took the opportunity to introduce herself to Mr. Patterson.

Nikki came out of the room, still crying, and hugged her dad. She looked at Chloe and said she had to get out of there. They left and Nikki drove Chloe straight home where she got out of the car and went right over to Ken's house.

Mrs. Wright answered the door and told Chloe that Ken couldn't see anyone. His fever had spiked to 104 degrees and he was in so much pain he couldn't get out of bed. He wasn't vomiting anymore because there was nothing left in his stomach. She told Chloe that the doctor thought he might have the flu, but they would have to wait it out for one more night. If he didn't get any better, then she was going to call the doctor again. At that point, Chloe decided it had been a long day and she better go home and get some sleep.

Bill and Sarah were home watching a movie; Sarah was asleep stretched out on the couch with her legs draped over Bill's lap. Chloe said hi and goodnight and went up to her room. She was exhausted. When she sat on her bed to take her shoes off, she saw the letters that were still typed out on the paper in the typewriter:

KENNETH

She had no recollection of them but she did remember waking up on her bedroom floor that morning and rushing out of the house because she was late. She started crying when she saw it. She couldn't help but think that might be the reason he is so sick. She stood up, put her hands on her face, and screamed, "NOOO!" She was crying violently. She heard her dad running up the stairs calling her name because he heard her. She through the white sheet over the typewriter so he wouldn't see it and opened the door to her bedroom to greet him.

"What is it, Chlo?" he asked, out of breath.

She lied: "Nothing. I saw a spider and it freaked me out. That's all. Sorry."

Satisfied with that he went back downstairs. She uncovered the Royal and sat at the desk chair. It was time to have a chat with that damned thing.

"What is happening?" she asked the piece of machinery. "Stop hurting people! Ken didn't do anything!"

She stared at it as if she expected a reply.

To her surprise, the keys started moving. She wasn't touching them, but she felt like they were in control of her. The keys started to plant letters on the same sheet of paper that was already loaded until it typed the words,

He Knows

Chloe decided she could play along with whatever game this typewriter was playing and she kept asking questions.

"What does he know?" she asked.

The keys went to work again.

About Raven

With those words, Chloe knew exactly what it was talking about. She had told Ken about the attack on Mrs. Patterson.

"Please don't hurt him!" she demanded. "He won't tell anyone! I swear! Please make him better!"

Can't

"I would not have told him if I thought he would tell anyone!" she screamed even louder. "DON'T FUCK-ING HURT HIM!"

Chloe got scared and covered it back up with the

sheet. She had lots of questions, but she would have to go about figuring them out a different way. Because of her, this typewriter had possibly killed two people, crippled one, and made another sick ... not to mention, it made her dog do something she would never do. She knew what she had to do: find out all she could about Mrs. Parrish and her relationship with everyone at the real estate office because it was *her* typewriter and some unexplained things happened back then too.

Chloe got a phone call from Mrs. Wright the following day. Kenneth's illness had turned into pneumonia and he was taken to the hospital. Upset at that news, Chloe told her that she would stop by the hospital later to see him. She decided to skip school that day and so she went over to Nikki's house because she couldn't go back home because her dad was still there. He would not be happy if he found out she skipped school. She wanted to talk to Nikki anyway about some things.

When she stepped up to Nikki's door, it opened before she had the chance to knock. Nikki was surprised to see Chloe as she stood in the doorway with swollen, bloodshot eyes. It was obvious to Chloe she had been crying. "Hi, Nikki. I am so sorry about your mom," Chloe said. "Can I talk to you about something?"

"I guess so." She let Chloe in the front door. There were still blood stains all over the front steps and walkway to her house; it looked like something out of a horror movie. Nikki brought Chloe back to her room. "What is it?"

Chloe looked around her room at all the pictures of her and Carol together. She didn't remember seeing all of those pictures the last time she was there. "I don't really know how to bring this up, but how much do you know about the time your mom worked at Humphrey's

Homes?"

"How do you know about that?" she asked. "I mean, how do you know where my mom used to work? You didn't even know her."

"Because my mom used to work there too," Chloe answered. "And the woman who died in the house I live in now, Mrs. Parrish, she worked there too. I actually came over here the other day and spoke with your mom about it and that's when she told me that she worked there a few years ago." She hoped Nikki wouldn't get upset that Chloe was over at her house when she was not there.

"Yeah, I knew about the Parrish woman. She was friends with my mom for a while, but then something changed. I know she didn't like my mom before she died."

"I think she was friends with *my* mom," Chloe said.

"What's your mom's name?" Nikki asked.

"Well, she died three years ago, but her name was Carissa Mattson."

Nikki's expression completely changed. She looked angry almost. "Oh, I remember her. She didn't like my mom either. As a matter of fact, the two of them used to gang up on my mother."

"Do you know much about Mrs. Parrish's life other than that?" Chloe asked.

"She was into some sort of witchcraft. She was always threatening my mom and then one day Mom got into a car accident. You know she used to have an old typewriter she used to cast her spells." As ridiculous as it sounded, Nikki was serious. "Well, I showed *her*. One day, I broke into her house and stole it."

"What did you do with it when you had it and how did she get it back there?" Chloe asked.

"I wanted to see what all the hype was about so I typed a couple things with it. But then, something happened," Nikki said.

"What do you mean?"

"I was just playing by typing a story about my mom's car. I hated that thing. She used to have this old beetle car from like the 80s or something. Anyway, I wrote about it getting into a wreck. A couple of weeks went by and then my mom got into an accident that totaled her car." Nikki started crying again. "She ended up being OK, but that car was destroyed and I couldn't help but think it was my fault, but I'm sure it was Mrs. Parrish who made it happen. I think she put a spell on the typewriter when it disappeared or something."

"How long did you keep the typewriter?" Chloe asked.

"For a while. I don't remember exactly because this was all like three years ago."

Chloe quickly changed her demeanor from total fixation on Nikki's words to anxiousness about having to leave all of the sudden. She assured Nikki she would be back soon; she just had to go see Ken at the hospital. She told Nikki how sick he had gotten and that she was worried about him.

Chloe walked home and saw Sarah's car in the driveway. She didn't realize how much time had passed but Sarah was home from school already. It was a half day anyway so Chloe figured she wasn't going to miss much by skipping. She went inside and asked Sarah if she could take her to the hospital. Sarah was happy to help her out and the two of them went to see Ken.

When they got to the hospital - a trip that was becoming all too familiar to Chloe - they stopped at the information desk. The same woman was there; she always seemed to be there each time Chloe went there. She told them Ken was in ICU and they could go up, but they probably would not be able to see him. They went up in hopes to just see someone related to him so they could find out how he was doing. They were actually surprised because both of his parents were there. Sgt. Wright always had to be at work so it was surprising to see him there. Sarah and Chloe walked up to them and Mrs. Wright gave Chloe a big welcoming hug right away and was crying.

"He needs a machine to help him breath," she said to Chloe. "The pneumonia has filled both of his lungs with fluid. I don't even know if he knows we are here." She was crying heavily at that point.

"Do you think I could see him?" Chloe asked.

"Yes. They are only letting one person in at a time and you have to get a mask from the nurse's station to wear inside his room." She showed Chloe where to go to get the mask.

Chloe went into the hospital room in the intensive care unit and Kenneth was lying there with his eyes closed. He was hooked up to all kinds of things. Once again, there was the sound of the breathing machine; it was taking breaths for Ken because he was having trouble breathing on his own. The heart monitor was beeping that rhythmic beat, which Chloe always thought was an eerie sound in hospitals. He looked cold and only had a single light blanket on him. Chloe peaked her head out the door and asked if he could have another blanket. His mom explained that they won't give him another one because he still has a fever and they don't want to raise his body temperature any more than it already is. It made sense but Chloe felt so bad for him. A week ago he was in her bed with her and now he lied in front of her helpless in a hospital bed. She pulled up a chair next to him and sat down.

"Ken? I hope you can hear me," she said as she took his hand in hers. "Please get better. I need you." She cried. She put her head down on his bed and stayed there for a while until a nurse came in and made her leave. She had to get his vitals.

Ken's parents were still standing outside the door. Mrs. Wright asked Chloe, "Are you alright, hun? It was so nice of you to come over to see him."

"What are they saying?" Chloe asked. "Is he going to get better?"

"They don't know yet. He is not responding to the medications and he hasn't woken up since we've been here this morning." Mrs. Wright said. "Just keep praying for him, okay?"

Chloe looked at her. "Of course I will." She wasn't much of a praying person, but she loved Ken and she did not want to lose him.

Chloe walked over to Sarah who just stood off in the distance. "We can go now if you want."

"Are you sure, Chlo?" Sarah asked. "We can stay as long as you need to."

"Yeah. I can't stand to see him this way," she cried and Sarah hugged her.

They went home and Chloe sat in the recliner chair in the living room and turned on the television. She didn't want to go up to her room, which was unusual. She just did not want to see that stupid typewriter and she didn't want to be alone.

After a couple of episodes of *The Big Bang Theory*, there was a loud knock on the front door. Chloe answered it and was surprised to see Nikki standing there in front of her. She asked Chloe to come outside for a minute.

"What's up?" Chloe asked.

"Did you go see Ken?" Nikki asked. "How is he?"

"I saw him, but he is not awake and he needs a breathing machine to help him breath." Chloe said. "He has pneumonia and it is pretty bad. They said his lungs are full of fluid."

"That sucks. I'm sorry," Nikki said. Then she abruptly changed the subject. "I have to ask *you* something now."

"What?"

"Is that old typewriter still here?" she asked.

"Why?" Chloe asked.

"Chloe, have you been using it?" Nikki's eyes got wide as she waited for an answer.

"Why are you asking me this?" Chloe asked again.

"If you are using it, you have to tell me. Chloe, it's evil. I thought the Parrish woman destroyed it, but if she didn't and it's here, you have to get rid of it!"

"Okay, Nikki, what do you know?" Chloe asked. She realized she had to be honest with Nikki at that point. "I have already tried to get rid of it twice. It won't let me!"

"Take me to it," Nikki said and Chloe took her inside to her room and showed it to her. She removed the sheet and the paper was still loaded with the threats against Ken. Nikki didn't say anything about it, although Chloe knew she saw it. "Oh my God! It looks just like I remember it."

"What did you expect?" Chloe asked. "Did you think it would change or something?"

"I don't know how you tried to get rid of it, but I burned it," Nikki said. "It doesn't look like it, does it? What have you done to get rid of it?"

Chloe answered, "I dumped it in a lake."

"My point exactly," Nikki said. "It doesn't look damaged at all. I don't know how to destroy it, but it needs to be destroyed. I am assuming that Piper's fall and Jill's accident had something to do with this thing?"

"No!" Chloe snapped.

"C'mon, Chloe. Tell me and then I will tell you what else I know," Nikki said.

"OK. All I know is that I came home to those girls' names typed on this paper." She pointed to where the current paper was with the writing on it about Ken. "I didn't type it. I swear!"

"Did you have something against them, like a grudge or something?" Nikki asked.

"They bullied me a lot because of the way I look, and I got into a fight with Piper at school. She would not leave me alone!" Chloe defended herself. "I never had a grudge, though. I don't waste my time holding grudges."

"You don't have to. This machine seems to latch onto whoever uses it. You must have typed something on it."

"Well, yeah." Chloe said. "I even ordered a new ribbon for it when I first found it. I just used it to type a little narrative report for English class." Chloe stopped abruptly. "Wait! I did see a similar story to the one I typed on the news a couple days later."

"That's what started it." Nikki said. "I did the same thing, but for a different reason. I heard Mrs. Parrish's stories came true and I wanted something bad to happen to someone who hurt my family. Anyway, I think I made it happen, and if I tell you what it was, then you can't get mad at me because I didn't know at the time what I was doing."

"You're scaring me, Nikki."

"It was three years ago and my mom worked at that real estate office. She was seeing this guy who made her happy. My dad was not in the picture yet; actually, he is my stepdad. Anyway, she talked about this guy all the time and he used to send her flowers and everything. Then one day she found out he was married because his wife confronted her at work. It was Carissa Mattson." Nikki looked into Chloe's eyes. "Your mom."

Chloe felt a shock wave run through her body when she heard her mom's name, but she kept listening.

"After that, my mom came home from work every day in tears because she said this woman would not leave her alone, even though she broke it off with her husband as soon as she found out they were married. My mom was not a homewrecker. It killed me to watch her go through this every day. That was about the time I stole Mrs. Parrish's typewriter. I wanted to hurt the woman who hurt my mom."

"It was you..." Chloe said. "My mom's accident!"

"Chloe, I swear I didn't know that would happen. I didn't know what I was doing and I didn't really believe in the typewriter until then." Nikki started crying. "I typed about a car accident after the company Christmas party. You have to understand. I was pissed. My mom didn't even go to the party because word spread around the office that she was a homewrecker. Everyone hated her and she was so depressed."

"Nikki, you killed my mom!" Chloe screamed.

"No, I didn't! That evil machine did it!" She yelled back as she pushed it with all of her strength onto the floor. It was so heavy it left an impression on the wooden floor. They both stood speechless until Chloe fell to her knees beside the Royal.

Every other thought escaped Chloe's mind as she thought of the tragic death of her mother and how she knew now that it was not necessary, and that it wasn't her dad's fault. She screamed at Nikki again, "What the hell is wrong with you?"

"Chloe, I was 14 and stupid. I didn't know any better and I didn't know you either." Nikki tried to explain.

"I was 14 too and I lost my mom because of what you did!" She was sobbing uncontrollably.

Sarah knocked at the door and asked if everything was okay before taking it upon herself to open it. She saw both girls in tears and the typewriter between them on the floor in pieces. "I think it's time for Nikki to go now," she said. The girls didn't say anything; Nikki just got up and walked out.

"What happened, Chloe?" Sarah asked.

"Nothing," Chloe said. "I'll take care of this mess."

Sarah seemed alright with that answer, or at least she did not want to push the subject any further, and she went out of the room and told Chloe to let her know if she needed anything.

Chloe cleaned up the pieces that had broken off the typewriter when it fell to the floor and she put them on the table. She was tired from her confrontation with

Nikki; her body was so exhausted from everything that was happening that she couldn't lift the body of it off the floor. She left it there and went downstairs. Raven was at the bottom of the steps. Chloe thought she probably heard the commotion upstairs and was afraid to go check it out. Chloe got her leash and took her outside for a walk so she could clear her head. She made sure to put her on a leash ever since the dog attack on Mrs. Patterson.

Before she knew it, she had walked to Nikki's street. She started thinking about her mom's accident again and what Nikki had told her. She didn't tell what she did to Nikki's mom though and her main concern now was Kenneth. Not knowing whether she would get the door slammed in her face or not, she walked over and knocked on the Patterson's door. Nikki answered it, almost immediately. She was still crying and her dad had not come home yet from the hospital where her mom lay lifeless.

"What do you want?"

"I'm sorry for freaking out on you like that," Chloe said. "I think we should pull together and try to decide what to do next because people are still getting hurt."

"I don't know what you think we can do," Nikki said. "And now I have a funeral to help my father plan."

"I'm sorry about that." Chloe took her hand. "This might sound crazy, but do you think it can be reversed?"

Nikki was confused for a moment. "Can what be reversed?" she asked.

"The bad things created by the typewriter," Chloe said.

"Chloe, listen to me." Nikki's voice was harsh. "Do not mess with that thing anymore! Mrs. Parrish knew what I did and kept telling me that she was going to fix it and then *she* died."

"She tried to help my mom?"

"They were friends and I know she wanted to but I don't know how far she got because she disappeared." Nikki said.

"Do you happen to know the date of Mrs. Parrish's disappearace?" Chloe asked. "If not, I can go look it up."

Nikki knew right away. "December 21, 2013."

Chloe's heart sank. That was the same day her mom got in that terrible car accident. Ken told her that Mrs. Parrish was trying to type something that night. She remembered Ken saying something about a word that was typed on the paper at the scene when Mrs. Parrish's house was searched. Knowing what her experience has been with the Royal, she was certain now that it had to have been her mother's name - Carissa - that was on the paper.

Chloe's mind was racing. She wondered if she could somehow save Ken. She asked Nikki if she would help her get the typewriter back up on her desk. Nikki agreed and they walked out the front door. They were greeted by Raven who was patiently waiting where Chloe left her tied to the railing by the front steps of the house. Nikki looked at Raven, gave her a pat on the head, and looked back at Chloe.

"Can I ask you something?" Nikki asked. "I mean, since we are getting everything out on the table and everything."

"Sure. What is it?"

Nikki looked as if she were searching for the words to fall from the sky. "Where was Raven the night of my mom's attack?"

Chloe burst into tears and Nikki's question was answered.

Nikki started crying also and they walked back to Chloe's house without saying another word to each other. They knew that they had basically killed each other's mothers.

Nikki spoke first when they got back to Chloe's room. "You know, my mom didn't know Bill was married," she said. "She thought *your* mom was the 'other' woman. That's why I was so mad at Carissa."

Chloe said, "Well, I thought their marriage was happy until I found out about your mom." She was still crying. "Can you imagine how I felt when I found out that we were neighbors? I met your mom and didn't realize who she was right away. I'm so sorry, Nikki. None of this should have ever happened."

"Let's just get rid of this thing once and for all!" Nikki said.

"I want to try to help Ken first."

"I don't know about this, Chloe." Nikki said. "However, if this thing kills me, I don't even care anymore."

233

"Don't say that!" Chloe cried.

"I don't want to be here without my mom, Chloe!"

"I'm pretty tired of not having my mom around either. I used to have lots of friends and get good grades in school, if you can believe that," Chloe said. "I haven't given a shit about anything, even my dad, since she died. I actually thought about killing myself a couple of times, but I'll be *damned* if I'm gonna let this machine do it!"

The two girls picked up the typewriter and gently placed it on top of Chloe's desk and sat on the bed to plot their next move.

36

Nikki was the first to go over to the Royal and she was surprised to find that the pieces that Chloe had gathered up earlier that broke off it when it was thrown on the floor were nowhere to be found. The plan was to put them back on the best they could, but Nikki looked everywhere and didn't see the pieces anywhere. From what she remembered it was just a few letter keys and a lever-looking thing that Nikki thought probably pushed the paper feeder roll from side to side. After crawling on the floor for few minutes, she gave up and told Chloe the pieces must be gone.

Chloe didn't look surprised. "Look on the typewriter," she said.

"What?" Nikki asked.

"Just look at it." Chloe knew they were probably there.

Nikki turned to Chloe. "What the hell?" The Royal was completely intact.

Chloe said, "Yeah, that thing fixes itself."

"What do you mean?" Nikki asked. "How can it do that?"

"I have had a couple of the keys break off and replace themselves on their own." Chloe said. "I thought I was losing my mind, but it happened." She walked over to where Nikki was standing and the room filled with a chill that caused both girls to hug themselves with their own arms for warmth.

"Why is it so cold in here?" Nikki asked.

"It gets like this from time to time, especially when I have the typewriter out."

"Maybe it's Mrs. Parrish," Nikki joked.

"It might be. I don't even think about it anymore," Chloe said. "I have never been afraid of ghosts or anything, and yes, I do believe in them. The problem I am having is with this typewriter. I'm not sure what the deal is with it. I mean, why does it feel like it is attached to me?"

"It's not just you," Nikki said. "I think it is whoever is using it at the time."

"OK, so what do we want to do?" Chloe asked. "My main concern here is Ken."

Just then, there was a knock at the door. Chloe opened it and Sarah was standing there with the cordless telephone in her hand. "It's Mrs. Wright, Chloe," she said. "Ken has taken a turn for the worst."

Chloe grabbed the phone and spoke with Mrs. Wright for less than a minute before she said, "I'll be right there." And she hung up the phone. "Nikki, I have to go to the hospital. Ken asked for me and is not doing so good. Can you take me there?"

Sarah interrupted. "I'll take you, hun." She knew Nikki had her own grieving to do because her mom had just died.

Leaving Nikki behind in Chloe's room, Sarah and

Chloe drove to the hospital; Chloe was crying the entire time. Sarah tried to talk to her to make her feel better, but she knew she couldn't make any promises that everything would be okay because it didn't sound good for Ken. He had asked to see Chloe, but then he slipped right back into unconsciousness and from what Mrs. Wright said, he crashed after that. He stopped breathing and they had to revive him. Chloe was so scared she wouldn't make it there before he died or slipped into a coma he would never wake up from. She had so much to say to him and felt like she was in a race against time to do so. They raced into the visitor's parking lot at the hospital and went right up to the intensive care unit. Chloe already knew where Ken's room was and Sarah could barely keep up with her as she ran to it. His parents were still there. Mrs. Wright sat in a chair outside his room with her head down in her hands. Chloe knew she was crying and she looked up when Chloe got there.

"Hi, Chloe. He wants to see you, but he is sleeping again," Mrs. Wright said. "Just go in and talk to him. They say he can hear us."

She handed Chloe a tissue to wipe her tears before she went in the room. Chloe stepped into the room where Ken didn't even look like he was alive. There was nothing but beeping, stillness, and silence. She slowly walked over to him and pulled up a chair. She did not know what to say to him so she just held his hand. A nurse came in and Chloe was surprised that she didn't make her leave.

"You must be Chloe," she said.

"Yes. How is he doing?"

The nurse shook her head slightly and said, "He's not doing too good but he did manage to speak and the only thing he kept saying was that he wanted to see you."

Chloe started crying and grabbed his hand tighter.

"Just talk to him," the nurse said. "I'll leave you alone. Let me know if you need anything."

Chloe rested her head down into her hand where Kenneth's hand was as well. She searched for the right words to say. "Ken?" She asked as if he would answer. "I'm here. I hope you can hear me." There was no movement or sound from him. She sat there for a while and before she knew it, a half hour had passed. Mrs. Wright came into the room and put her hand on Chloe's shoulder.

"Hun, why don't you go get some coffee or something?" she said. "I'll sit with him."

"Okay." Chloe was afraid to leave in case something happened so she quickly got Sarah and they went to the snack bar and got a soda for Chloe and a coffee for Sarah. "Thanks for bringing me here," she said to Sarah.

"It's no problem. You know I am here for you, right?" Sarah asked.

"Yeah, I know," Chloe said. "Sometimes my mind doesn't let me admit that though and I am sorry about that."

"I know, Chloe," Sarah said. "It's okay. Let's get back." They walked back to the ICU and Chloe relieved Mrs. Wright again.

Chloe looked around at the machines that appeared to be keeping Ken alive and prayed that they would just keep beeping. She knew as long as they were making noise he was alive, at least she thought that was how it worked. She reached over and grabbed Ken's hand again. This time she had no intension of letting go... ever. Mentally exhausted from everything that had happened over the last couple of days, Chloe put her head down again to rest it on the side of Ken's hospital bed and she dozed off. She was awakened by another tap on her shoulder. It was the nurse that was taking care of him.

"There is someone outside that is asking for you," she said.

"Who is it?" Chloe asked her.

"I don't know. It is a man and he says you are his daughter's friend."

Chloe went out of the room with the nurse and was surprised to see Nikki's dad standing there. She didn't even know his name. "Hi, Mr. Patterson," she said.

"Hi, Chloe. Have you seen Nikki?" he asked.

"I was with her earlier, but then I came here and I assumed she went home," Chloe said.

Mr. Patterson looked distraught. "I had to stay here to clear up some loose ends and now I can't get a hold of her. I have called her cell a few times and the house phone. She's not answering either one of them."

Chloe could tell he was worried. "I will try to call her." Chloe took her cell phone out of her pocket and hit Nikki's name. It rang four times before voicemail picked it up. Chloe left a message telling Nikki to call her as soon as she got the message. Mr. Patterson thanked Chloe and said he was going to go home and that he would let her know if he heard from Nikki. He said he was worried because she was not handling her mother's death well. Chloe thanked him and said she was sorry for the loss of his wife. Then she went back into Kenneth's room where there was no change in scenery. Not that she thought there would be; she went back to her seat and held his hand. If he was going to die, then she would not let him do it alone. She needed him to know she was there.

The nurse came in again after a while and said visiting hours were over but she would let Chloe stay because he asked for her earlier. Chloe thanked her and put her hand on his forehead to brush his hair aside. She wanted to see his face. His eyes were closed, but he was beautiful. His face was pale, but he looked so peaceful and she leaned forward toward him and gently kissed his cheek.

"Ken, please don't leave me just when I found you," she whispered just as Mrs. Wright walked back into the room.

"Chloe? May I have a moment alone with him please?" she asked.

Chloe got up to walk out even though she didn't want to leave his side. "Sure," she said as she went out into the hall where Sgt. Wright was standing.

"How are you doing?" he asked her.

"Okay, I guess," she said. She was surprised he was talking to her after the way he interrogated her at the station. "I just want him to get better."

"We all do," he said. Then he went over to the nurse's station to talk to them about something that Chloe couldn't hear.

The silence and tension in the hallway was broken by the sudden cry of Mrs. Wright coming from inside Kenneth's room. "Ben! Get in here!" she yelled.

He ran into the room and Chloe followed close behind. She wanted to see what was going on, even though she thought the worst.

"Look!" Mrs. Wright pointed to Ken's hand, the one that Chloe was holding. His fingers were moving. The Wrights and Chloe stared in amazement as the nurse called for his doctor.

"Ken!" Mrs. Wright said to him. "Can you hear us? Please come back to us, baby!" She went over and held his hand until the doctor came in.

Ken's nurse came in with the on-call doctor and they took his vitals.

"I don't believe it," the doctor said. "They are normal and he is breathing on his own." He went over to the respirator machine and turned it off. Ken's parents were nervous at this because he had not been able to breath for about 24 hours and they said he was getting worse. When the machine was turned off, Ken took a deep breath and continued to breathe all by himself. The doctor said his blood pressure was also normal and he could not explain any of it. Ken was still not awake, but he was stable. The doctor asked everyone to leave the room so he could give him a thorough exam without interruption.

Everyone waited out in the hall; the Wrights just held each other and cried while Chloe sat in a chair next to them, anxious to get back in the room to see her boyfriend.

After a short time, the doctor came out and told Chloe that Ken was awake and asking for her, and *only* her. She went back in and his eyes were open. He still looked weak, but he was awake. She grabbed his hand and kissed it.

"Thank God!" she said.

"Are you okay?" Ken asked. "You look like you were crying."

"I was," Chloe said. "I thought I lost you."

"You didn't lose me, but what happened?" Ken asked. "The last thing I remember is going to the real estate office."

"You don't remember anything else?" Chloe asked. "Like getting sick? Ken, you were so sick and throwing up."

"I don't remember that," he said. "I don't even remember coming here. I just remember waking up a few minutes ago to see you." He reached for her hand.

"I had to come. They were saying you might not pull through this," she said. "They said you had a bad case of pneumonia. How do you feel now?"

"I'm not sure. I am a little warm actually." He moved the blanket off the lower part of his body. "And my gown and sheets are wet."

"You had a high fever. You must have sweat it out of you," Chloe said. "Your mom said you were in a lot of pain; so much that you couldn't get out of bed and she couldn't touch you without you pulling away."

"Everything feels fine now." Ken was puzzled. "I really don't remember any of that."

His nurse came over to him and stuck a thermometer in his mouth, completely halting his conversation with Chloe. She held it there for a few seconds until it beeped and she studied the numbers it displayed. "It's normal," she said. "98.6 degrees. How is this possible?" she asked the doctor.

"You know how it works, Becky. There are no guaranteed prognoses in medicine." Chloe thought his response was code for, *I have no idea.*

Mrs. Wright stood on the side of his bed opposite Chloe and burst into tears. "Are you really okay? We were so worried."

"Mom, really, I feel fine," he answered. "I just feel like I have been asleep for a long time so I am tired and I seriously need a shower." Chloe and Mrs. Wright laughed and Ken looked at his nurse and asked her if he could try to get out of bed.

"Let me help you," she said.

"No. I can do it." Ken held Chloe's hand the whole time as he swung his legs over the side of the bed and slowly stood up. He was noticeably wobbly and Chloe helped him to the bathroom where he went in and shut the door.

Nurse Becky stood outside the bathroom door listening while Ken peed for what seemed like five minutes. After the toilet flushed, he peeked his head out of the door and asked his mom if he had any clean clothes to change into so he could take a shower. Nurse Becky interrupted him and told him she would get him another gown and told him that he would have to stay dressed in a gown as long as he was still admitted as a patient. He agreed and she got him a clean hospital gown. While he took a shower, Mrs. Wright went out in the hall to speak with the doctor. She came back in and told Chloe they were going to get him some solid food and if he could hold it down after eating it, they would let him go home the next day. Nobody could believe how quickly things were happening.

Just then they heard Sgt. Wright's pager go off. He was out in the hall speaking with some nurses. There was a call for a possible suicide. He came into Kenneth's room and explained that he had to leave because they were short-staffed at the station. He told Ken he would stay if he needed him. Ken told him he would be okay, that there were enough people there to take care of his needs. He leaned over Ken's bed and gave his son a tight hug and held him for a few moments as close as he could without feeling like he would hurt him. Ken was still so weak. He then gave his wife a kiss and made her promise to call him if anything changed. He could be back in five minutes in his police cruiser. She agreed and he left the room.

Chloe went out in the hallway to ask Sarah if she could spend the night at the hospital with Ken. She told her to ask the nurses. She did and the nurses said she could but there was no place for her to sleep but the uncomfortable chair she was sitting in. That was fine with her; she just didn't want to leave Ken's side. She told Sarah she could go and she would call her in the morning or during the night if she needed to get home. Sarah gave her a hug, kissed her on the forehead, and left the hospital.

Chloe went back into Ken's room and plopped into the chair that would be her bed for the night. She decided to take that opportunity to call Nikki again. The phone rang a few times and went to voicemail, *"This is Nikki. You know what to do."* Chloe thought she could be asleep or just ignoring calls. Just like Chloe, Nikki went through periods when she just wanted to be left alone and she was going through a lot so this was nothing out of the ordinary as far as Chloe was concerned. She did leave a message, but didn't expect a return call.

Ken was freshly showered and back in bed. "Now I feel better," he said. "I just needed to get the hospital gunk off me." He and Chloe laughed. She got up from the chair and gave him a kiss. "You look tired," he said.

"I am a little. There has been a lot going on," she said.

"Why don't you try to go to sleep?" he asked her. "It's getting late and nothing is going to happen to me. I don't want you getting sick now."

Chloe agreed and got into a comfortable position in the chair. It took some maneuvering but she finally got into a position she could deal with. Ken and his mom continued to talk in low voices so Chloe could rest, but her slumber was quickly interrupted by her cell phone, which rang out with the Adams Family ringtone. She had set up that ringtone for whenever Sarah called her. She looked at the caller ID on the screen and it was confirmed. Sarah had just left her a little while ago and was already calling her. She ignored the call, but it only took two minutes for Sarah to call again. Chloe answered that time because she thought it must be important.

"Hello?"

"Chloe!" Sarah was on the other end of the line. "Something has happened! You need to come home. Is there someone there who can drive you?"

"I'm not sure," Chloe said. "Ken just woke up so his mom might not want to leave but I can check. What is going on?"

"Just try to get home!" Sarah said. "If you have trouble, call me back."

"Okay, but you're scaring me. Is it Dad?" Chloe asked.

"No. Your father is fine."

Chloe ended the call and looked at Mrs. Wright with a worried look on her face.

"What's wrong Chloe?" Mrs. Wright asked.

"I have to get home, but I don't have a car," she said.

Ken interrupted and said that his mom should drive her home because he wanted her to pick him up a few things from home anyway. Mrs. Wright agreed and went out to the nurses' station to let them know she was going to leave for a bit, but she gave them instructions to call her immediately if anything happened.

Chloe told Ken she would be back also and then she and Mrs. Wright left the hospital and headed home. Ken's mom looked like she could use a shower also and a change of clothes. When they got to her car, she opened the passenger side door for Chloe to get in first. She tried to call her husband before pulling out of the lot, but no luck. Her call went straight to voicemail. She just wanted to let him know she was leaving the hospital for a bit.

The ten-minute car ride felt a lot longer to Chloe because she did not really know Ken's mom well and couldn't think of anything to talk to her about, not to mention the fact that Chloe was so curious and worried and wondered why it seemed to be an emergency for her to get home. She also knew the only thing on Mrs. Wright's mind was her son and she knew that she did not want to leave the hospital in the first place.

Mrs. Wright finally broke the silence. "Thank you for coming out to the hospital, Chloe. We really appreciate it and I know it made Kenneth happy."

"It's no problem. I wanted to be there and I am so glad he's okay," Chloe said as they approached their street.

They turned the corner onto Honeysuckle Drive and their conversation was cut short by a noticeable commotion going on up the road. The flashing of bright red and blue lights was everywhere. As they got closer to it they noticed there were six or seven police cars, as well as an ambulance in the road ahead of them. Mrs. Wright sped up a little and as they approached the scene, Chloe realized all the vehicles were parked in a scattered formation in front of her house and the Wrights' house. She immediately got scared and Mrs. Wright, without warning, stepped on the gas to propel them into her driveway causing Chloe's head to jerk backwards and hit the headrest of her seat. She shook it off and quickly regained her focus on what was happening because she now could see that all of the uproar was at *her* house. She quickly got out of the car and ran over to her front door where she was stopped by the outstretched arm of a police officer who stood in the doorway.

"Miss, you can't go in there," he said.

"This is my house! What happened?" Chloe demanded to know.

Sarah appeared in the doorway behind the deputy and reached around him to take hold of Chloe's hand. "It's okay, Officer. She lives here."

She took Chloe inside and told her to have a seat on the sofa while she tried to reach Bill again. Apparently, she had been trying to call him with no luck. He was at an old friend's house that night looking at his car. She hung up the phone and sat down next to Chloe on the sofa. She had been crying and Chloe was real scared because no one had told her what was going on yet.

Finally, Sarah spoke. "Chloe, was there anyone in the house when you left to go see Ken tonight?" She asked.

"What do you mean?" Chloe asked. "Is Raven okay?"

"Yes. The police have her locked in one of their cars because of all the excitement."

"Sarah, what the hell is going on?" Chloe yelled.

Chloe looked around the house and noticed that none of the officers were inside. There must have been twelve police officers there, but they were all outside, which she thought was strange.

"Calm down, Chloe," Sarah said. "I'm not sure what happened, but..."

Chloe stopped her. "Nikki!"

"What?" Sarah asked.

"My friend Nikki. She was here when I left. I figured she just went home!" Chloe looked in the direction of the stairs. "No! Oh no, no, no..." She left Sarah and ran upstairs.

Instead of following her, Sarah told one of the officers that she went upstairs and that she was worried about what she might find up there. The officers didn't even let Sarah go up there so she had no idea what Chloe might run into.

Chloe got to her room and there was another policeman at her bedroom door who she pushed and struggled with until she broke past him. Once she was past him, the bedroom door slammed shut trapping him on the other side.

It was freezing cold in there and she noticed the window was open. She saw some papers right away that caught her attention. They were scattered on the floor. She dropped to her knees and tried desperately to put them together in any kind of order that might make sense. She was not quite sure what the pages were until she gathered them all up in her hands. She quickly skimmed some of it because she knew she didn't have much time before the deputies forcefully threw her out of there. The papers were pages that were typed by someone; it appeared to be about a boy with the flu. She read as the pages talked about individual symptoms of the flu and how they miraculously got better. It was obvious the writing was about Kenneth. The only explanation she could come up with was that Nikki must have typed it, which made sense because Chloe was talking to her about wanting to use the typewriter to make Kenneth better.

Chloe forgot about all of the commotion downstairs for a moment as a wave of chilly air brushed through her like a phantom hand and whisked the papers right back out of her hands and strewn them all over the room. They stayed in the air and formed a funnel like a tornado as they spun around just inches from the floor. That sent a chill up Chloe's spine as she slowly turned her head toward her desk, only to see that the typewriter was covered up by its sheet. She did not remember covering it up so she figured Nikki did it. Curious if there was another page in it about Ken, she yanked the sheet off of it and, just at that second, her window slammed shut causing it to shatter throwing shards of glass everywhere. Chloe jumped and just stared at everything that was happening like she was in shock. Her attention was brought back to the Royal typewriter. She felt like her heart literally stopped for a second as she read the single word that was typed on the paper in the typewriter's all-too-familiar capital letters.

N I K K I

Chloe looked from the window back to the papers and realized it *had* to be Nikki. She was the reason Ken got better so fast. They wondered if the curses or whatever they were could be reversed and Nikki must have wanted to test that theory.

Chloe's mind temporarily went back to the hospital where Sgt. Wright got the call about a possible suicide. She screamed and ran to her broken window and looked down at the ground below. She discovered where all of the police officers were. They were gathered around Nikki's mangled body.

"NO!" Chloe screamed and slammed her hands down on the windowsill. Her hands were cut instantly by the leftover shards of glass which remained in the window frame. Not caring about the blood that began to spill out over both of her arms, Chloe ran away from the window and out of her room pushing past the police officer who just stood in her doorway as if he were frozen.

She ran down the steps so fast she almost tumbled to the bottom as her feet barely grazed the tops of the bottom four steps. Sarah tried to stop her but was unsuccessful as Chloe made it to the back door and went outside just as the coroner showed up. He pronounced Nikki dead and covered her up with a black tarp before

Chloe had a chance to see her.

Chloe saw Mr. Patterson sitting on the ground nearby, but she was afraid to go talk to him; he looked so distraught. She wondered if he even really realized what was happening as he had not yet come to terms with the passing of his wife and now his daughter was dead.

A police officer introduced himself to Chloe as Deputy Matthews. He asked if it was okay if he asked her a few questions. She agreed and they went inside and sat at the kitchen table.

"Were you friends with the deceased, Miss Mattson?" he asked.

"Yes, and her name is Nikki." Chloe said. She did not like it that Deputy Matthews referred to Nikki as "the deceased."

"Okay. Do you know why Nikki was here all by herself in your house?" he asked.

Chloe was crying. "We were hanging out and then I got a phone call. I left to go see my boyfriend in the hospital. He was real sick and I got word that his condition changed." Chloe said. "I left and thought Nikki was going to just go home."

Deputy Matthews took notes of what Chloe said. "Do you know any reason she may have wanted to take her own life?"

Chloe knew that this had to do with that stupid typewriter, but she couldn't tell him that. He would never believe her. "Her mom just died and she was pretty upset about it. She wasn't handling it very well. I should have never left her alone!" Chloe cried.

"This is not your fault, Miss Mattson," Matthews said and he got up from the table.

Sarah went into the kitchen to see if Chloe needed anything and she made some hot tea for herself. The cops were searching the entire property for any clues of what might have happened. Chloe had an idea of what could have happened, but had to wait for everyone to leave so she could deal with it in her own way. She just sat at the kitchen table with her hands folded and her eyes fixated on them. The longer she sat there waiting for everyone to clear out, the more upset she was getting.

She got up and looked out the back window. She saw Deputy Matthews questioning Nikki's dad as he sobbed into his folded hands. Chloe had never seen a man cry like that before. It was understandable and she felt so bad for him because he had just lost more than one person should ever lose in one day. Chloe looked to where Nikki's body was lying cold on the ground and noticed they were finally putting her on a gurney to get her out of there.

Bill Mattson finally showed up to his house. He frantically ran about searching for Chloe because all of the emergency vehicles made him think something happened to her. He found her hysterically crying in the kitchen. She jumped up and hugged him like she would never let him go.

"Chloe, what happened?" he asked. "Are you okay?"

Sarah walked into the kitchen and filled him in on the events of the evening. He explained that he left his phone in his car while he was at his friend's house and that was why she could not get a hold of him. He apologized to both of them and went outside to talk to Sgt. Wright who was speaking with the coroner.

The area started to clear out and Chloe saw cop car after cop car drive away. Nikki's body was removed and they brought Raven back inside the house. Chloe watched all of the emergency personnel drive away in their flashy vehicles while the nosey neighbors slowly headed back into their homes; then, she knew what she had to do.

Chloe asked Bill and Sarah if Raven could stay downstairs for the night since the window in her bedroom was broken. She knew the window gave a somewhat believable reason for the dog not to be upstairs on that particular night. They tried to convince her not to stay in her room either, but she insisted on being in her room where she could mentally process everything that happened. She proceeded to convince them that she needed to be in the place she had spent her last moments with Nikki. Although they were not completely onboard with the idea, they could not argue with her. She had been through so much in the last 24 hours.

On her way to her room, she saw Bill's toolbox at the bottom of the steps. She figured he must have left if there due to all the commotion when he got home, so she opened it and took his hammer out. She glanced upward toward the top of the stairs before slowly climbing up them, one at a time as if she was in no hurry. Her face was pale and had no expression on it whatsoever with eyes that were like those of a demon as she stared straight out in front of her at what seemed to be nothing. She held the hammer down at her side as it dangled from her hand grazing her leg with each step.

Chloe reached the top of the staircase after what seemed to be an eternity and continued down the corridor and into her bedroom, never letting her eyes falter from the direction she was headed. She never blinked, she did not miss a step, and she did not hesitate when she came upon her bedroom door. She just walked right in, turned around, and locked the door behind her. She continued her trancelike walk over to the shattered window where there was a slight cool breeze blowing in that instantly sent a chill up her spine. She looked out the window to make sure there wasn't anyone left in the backyard tying up some loose ends or anything. Then she went over to her desk where she planned to end all of the pain in her life once and for all. She stood in front of the machine for a few minutes just peering through it as if she were trying to read its inner-most thoughts. Tears welled up in both of her eyes as her face heated up to the point she felt it would catch fire. She felt a powerful force within her that she never felt before. It was as if she was taken over by something else. She didn't know what it was; she only knew that it was strong.

Without time to get ahold of her immediate emotions she took a long deep breath, reached behind her with the hand that held the hammer, and with every ounce of strength she could muster up inside of her she swung it over her head and straight into the center of the keyboard of the typewriter sending a handful of its keys along with some tiny pieces of metal and debris into the air in every direction until they fell down to the floor and surrounded the area where she stood.

Chloe continued to glare upon the typewriter with a hatred so strong she could not control her next move as she reached behind her back again with the hammer before propelling it forward and slamming it into the evil that had become her worst enemy. This time the blow caused more pieces of the Royal to scatter throughout the room. Unsatisfied with the destruction so far because she felt the machine was not fully demolished, Chloe gathered up all of the fear inside of her and partnered it with all of her anger and centered it all on her arm, and she developed a strength so strong she was able to swing her arm over her head with a lot more force. This time, the hammer's head smashed directly down into the center of the paper roller with such force the machine was knocked to the floor and her desk now had a large crack down the center of it.

Chloe turned her gaze from the forward trance it had been in and looked down at the wreckage that had fallen two feet away from where she was standing, where the impact had caused such a blow to its inner mechanism that metal shards had flown all around her.

When its tiny remains made their downward plunge, Chloe's face and upper body became the landing platform on which they planted themselves. Sharp fragments of machinery cut deep into the flesh of her cheeks and arms. It seemed to her that the shower of machine parts was never-ending as they fell in a constant stream from above her head. Lacerations continued to appear all over her body until she could no longer stand. She fell to the floor in a pool of blood that had spilled from her own veins.

On her knees she was able to find enough strength to give the Royal one last blow to its base, which resulted in the hammer punching a hole into the metal base.

Instantly, a beam of bright light protruded out of the opening that was as bright as the surface of the sun and it shined straight up to the ceiling, where it planted a perfect circle in the center of the room. Chloe had to shield her eyes from it as she tried to look at it. On her knees, bleeding and weak she looked as if she were praying as she struggled to figure out exactly what was happening as the remaining pieces of metal raised off the floor around her. She just stared at the mechanism as they started re-entering the typewriter through the hole she had made with the hammer. Chloe was unable to move as the horror from the scene flooded into her.

Without warning, a strong gust of wind blew into the unshielded window and surrounded Chloe with shards of glass from its broken window. Suffering more deep wounds from cuts that slashed her skin during this bedroom wind storm, she looked down at her arms, took a deep breath, and mustered up the loudest, blood curdling, high pitched scream it seemed any human could ever make as she was hoisted into the air by an invisible force and thrown against the wall. She fell, tried to get to her feet, and was immediately picked up and tossed back toward the direction she had come from.

This supernatural war continued on as Bill came running up the stairs and pounded on Chloe's door without any success in obtaining entry. Desperate and concerned for his daughter, he called his neighbor, Sgt. Wright, who quickly made his way back over to the Mattson home. By the time Bill let Sgt. Wright into the house and brought him up to Chloe's room, the commotion had stopped. Bill banged repeatedly on the door again but got no answer from the other side as Sarah just stood off to the side hysterically crying. Both men tried their hand at getting an answer from the inside of Chloe's bedroom, but when Sgt. Wright threatened to break the door down and they still heard nothing from Chloe, he made good on his threat. After asking Bill and Sarah to stand back, Sgt. Wright hoisted one leg in the air and kicked the bedroom door in the old fashioned way.

To their surprise, there was no one on the other side. The room was in disarray with glass everywhere, but Chloe was nowhere to be found. They rushed over to the open window space to see if Chloe had jumped out the window, but they saw nothing and no one on the ground below. The three of them turned to look the room over one more time.

All that was there was glass on the floor, an unmade bed, and a desk with a newly refurbished Royal typewriter on it. Bill did notice the typewriter had a single sheet of paper protruding out of the top of it so he walked over to it to get a closer look. When he was close enough to the desk to see what was typed on the sheet of paper, he gasped and grabbed his chest. There was one single word displayed in black ink:

C H L O E